W9-AXW-238

SPIDER-MAN®

WANTED
DEAD OR ALIVE

WANTED
DEAD OR ALIVE

CRAIG SHAW GARDNER

ILLUSTRATIONS BY BOB HALL

BYRON PREISS MULTIMEDIA COMPANY, INC.

NEW YORK

A BOULEVARD/PUTNAM BOOK
PUBLISHED BY
G. P. PUTNAM'S SONS
A MEMBER OF PENGUIN PUTNAM INC.
NEW YORK

A Boulevard/Putnam Book
Published by G. P. Putnam's Sons
Publishers Since 1838
a member of Penguin Putnam Inc.
200 Madison Avenue
New York, NY 10016

Byron Preiss Multimedia Company, Inc.
24 West 25th Street
New York, NY 10010
www.byronpreiss.com

Special thanks to Ginjer Buchanan, Michelle LaMarca,
Emily Epstein, Howard Zimmerman, Mike Thomas,
Steve Behling, and Ursula Ward

Copyright © 1998 Marvel Characters, Inc.

Edited by Keith R.A. DeCandido and Steve A. Roman
Interior design by Michael Mendelsohn of MM Design 2000, Inc.

All rights reserved. This book, or parts thereof,
may not be reproduced in any form without permission.
Requests for such permissions should be addressed to:
Byron Preiss Multimedia Company, Inc.
24 West 25th Street
New York, NY 10010

Library of Congress Cataloging-in-Publication Data

Gardner, Craig Shaw.
Spider-man: wanted dead or alive / Craig Shaw Gardner;
illustrations by Bob Hall.
p.   cm.
"A Boulevard/Putnam book."
ISBN 0-399-14385-8
I. Hall, Bob. ill.   II. Title.
PS3557.A7116S65   1998   97-53226 CIP
813'.54—dc21

Printed in the United States of America
1   3   5   7   9   10   8   6   4   2

I'm old enough to remember a time when you really had to work to find comic books; when they were handled exclusively by magazine distributors, when they would sell out in a day or two of showing up at your local drugstore or newsstand, and sometimes they wouldn't show up at all. That all changed with the advent of the direct market (opened by Phil Seuling some twenty-five years back) and the first stores that specialized in the glorious graphic art of comics. At last, a place where I belonged!

This book is dedicated to one of the great comic shops (including all those who have toiled therein):

The Million Year Picnic

and independent comic book stores everywhere. Long may you sell!

ACKNOWLEDGMENTS

Thanks and a tip o' the webbing go to Keith R.A. DeCandido, Steve Roman, Merrillee Heifetz, and the usual suspects—Rich, Jeff, Mary, Victoria, and especially Barbara, who all helped shepherd this sometimes unruly book to publication. And let's not forget Stan Lee and Steve Ditko, who first showed me, some thirty-odd years ago, that a super hero could have even more problems than I had.

Prologue

His spider-sense had been tingling for a good reason. Spider-Man wasn't quite sure if the scene below was a bank robbery or a war zone. Either way, it had ground traffic to a halt on Park Avenue.

The action took place in the Mid-Pacific Bank's plaza at the corner of Fortieth Street. It was one of those open-air atriums with a fountain in the middle that architects always seemed to design for skyscrapers.

The four guys walking stiffly across the plaza were armed to the teeth and wore black ski masks, jeans, and bulky sweatshirts—Spider-Man figured they wore Kevlar under the sweatshirts. The two in the lead carried Uzis; the third carried a forty-four Magnum in each hand and sported a belt hung with a half-dozen grenades; the last one balanced a long, pipelike device on his shoulder that looked like some cross between a bazooka and a rocket launcher. They were so overloaded with gear, they looked like they were doing a photo shoot for *Soldier of Fortune.*

Each carried a loaded backpack, too. Since they were leaving one of the largest banks in Manhattan, Spidey hoped the packs were filled only with money, rather than more instruments of destruction. They might have used that rocket launcher to blow a hole in the bank vault. Spidey hadn't heard an explosion, but the city was noisy enough to mask it, especially if the vault was underground. If one had enough guts and enough firepower, anything was possible. But just because they had gotten in didn't mean they'd be able to get away.

Especially if Spider-Man had anything to say about it.

Time to get to work, he thought, *in more ways than one.* He quickly set up his camera, the spanking-new remote-controlled Minolta, in an unobtrusive corner to get some photos of the action. It was a beautiful piece of machinery, fitted with a wide-angle lens that would catch just about anything. Since, as Peter Parker, he made his living taking crime photos for the New York *Daily Bugle,* with a specialty in action shots of Spider-Man, it behooved him to get pictures of what looked to be a pretty daring, and therefore newsworthy, daytime robbery.

His wife, Mary Jane Watson-Parker, had bought Peter this baby after the latest residual check came in from her voice-over work on *The GigaGroup* animated series. After all, she pointed out, if he was going to be the next photographer to win a Pulitzer prize he needed to upgrade his equipment. His previous camera had taken quite a beating over the past few months and was starting to fall apart. As for the one he normally wore on his belt, that had been trashed by those ninja-style crooks he'd fought the day before. They had got in only one good kick, but it was right to his camera.

After setting up the new camera's automatic timer, he quickly turned to the drama below.

The four overarmed crooks were attracting a crowd. It was a typical New York reaction. *"What'd you do for lunch today?" "Oh nothing much. Took a walk. Got a hot dog. Watched a bank robbery."*

Quite a mob had gathered, maybe a hundred strong, around the edges of the plaza. At least everybody was hanging back, with nobody trying to be the hero. Spidey guessed that left the job open for him.

The four gunmen stopped midway across the plaza. They stared out at the crowd. The crowd stared back. There was a long moment of silence.

Spider-Man would have to figure out the best way to catch all four of them before anybody could get hurt.

"Hey, Victor?" the first man called back. "What are we gonna do?"

"Just keep walking, Richie," the man with the rocket launcher said from the rear. "With this kind of firepower, no one's gonna stop us."

Richie nodded and took a couple of hesitant steps forward. The crowd shifted around again, a couple of people pointing, a couple of voices raised in alarm, but nobody really moved. Richie stopped again. Apparently, he hadn't thought about shooting civilians.

"Jeff! Marty!" Victor called. "Get up there with Richie! If anybody gets in our way, mow 'em down!"

"Ah, boys, don't you know by now," Spider-Man called from where he hung on the wall, "we New Yorkers just want to be friendly! How about a group hug?"

Everybody looked up at that.

"It's Spider-Man!" Richie called.

Somebody always said that.

"You were expecting someone else?" he called down as he shot a line of webbing to the far side of the plaza. "You try to conquer the world, you get the Avengers or the Fantastic Four. You rob a bank, you get Spider-Man. It's in my contract."

He swung quickly over the heads of the bank robbers. They spun around after him, trying to get a bead on him with their fancy arsenal.

So far, this was working according to plan. Constant movement and snappy patter kept the bad guys focused on Spidey rather than innocent bystanders. While it was a lot less flashy than his webbing or his super strength, sometimes the patter worked just as well.

"Out of my way!" Victor yelled to his cohorts. "Let's see how Spider-Freak handles a rocket in his belly!"

Spider-Man stopped as he reached the wall over the bank. This would never do. Even pointed in the air, the rocket launcher could seriously damage one of the surrounding buildings and shower rubble on the street below. As far as Spider-Man was concerned, that kind of mayhem wasn't allowed.

As soon as Victor lifted the rocket launcher his way, Spidey lifted his right fist and sent off one well-aimed stream of web-fluid from the nozzle hidden at his wrist.

Bull's-eye, he thought, grinning under his full face mask. A glob of webbing covered the rocket launcher's muzzle.

Victor staggered back, pulled the pipe from his shoulder, and stared into the now-clogged opening.

"Okay, guys," Spider-Man said. "Fun time's over. So, do I pick you off one by one, or do you want to go as a group?"

The other three guys started shouting at each other. The two with Uzis pointed their weapons at Spider-Man, but the guy with the Magnums was waving his guns at the crowd.

The bank alarm started.

Oh, great. Just the thing for three nervous guys with guns. Better get this over with now.

"Coming in for a landing!"

He jumped into their midst, as nimble as a spider. The flashy stuff was over. It was time to use his fists. He knocked over the first two guys before they could even swing their Uzis around. One of them—Richie—skidded all the way across the plaza.

"Yeah, Spider-Man!" somebody shouted.

"Go get 'em, Spidey!"

"Show them you can't wave a gun around in New York City!"

Nice to see that the crowd's with me for a change. Too many times in his career, he'd be in the middle of a fight and the bystanders would be clamoring for his head as much as the crooks'.

The guy with the Magnums turned toward him then.

"I'm waiting for you, Marty," Spider-Man said. "Or was it Jeff? We never were properly introduced."

"I'll introduce *you,* Spider-Man!" Jeff (or Marty) shouted at the top of his lungs as he raised both guns to fire.

But Spidey's webbing was already on its way, two strands this time, one encasing each of the gunman's hands, gun included. Marty (or Jeff) stumbled forward, his arms encased in web cocoons up to his elbows. "I'll get you, you freak, you hear!" he screamed as he fell to his knees.

He wouldn't be shooting anything until the mass of webbing dissolved, but of course by then he'd be in police custody. Spidey could already hear sirens growing louder. Time to finish up here and get out of the crowd.

"That's what I call the two-fisted approach," Spider-Man said.

"Hey, Victor," the guy on his knees said. "Kill him for me."

What's he talking about? Spidey spun around.

The guy with the rocket launcher had staggered to his feet and was hoisting the pipe back onto his shoulder.

"This thing can take out a tank," Victor said. "Don't worry, guys. I'll blow out the webbing and blow away Spider-Man."

But Spider-Man knew better. His webbing had defeated, and demolished, weapons far more powerful than a black-market rocket launcher. "You shoot that now, it'll blow up in your face."

"Yeah. So you say. You're not going to fool me this time!"

Victor banged the pipe a couple of times with the heel of his hand, as if that might dislodge the webbing. Spidey had seconds to act before the thing would blow up in Victor's face, kill him instantly, and spread deadly shrapnel throughout the crowd.

Spider-Man took a running jump, somersaulted in midair, and landed on Victor feetfirst just as the thief's finger started to twitch on the firing button. The rocket launcher fell from Victor's hands as he landed on his back, out cold.

Suddenly, Spider-Man felt the buzz of his spider-sense, warning him that, despite the way it looked, the crisis was not over.

"You're not done with us yet, bug!"

Spidey whirled to see that it was Richie, somehow back on his feet across the plaza. Spider-Man thought he had knocked the gunman cold. The body armor must have absorbed some of the blow.

"I'll get back to you," Spider-Man said as he grabbed the rocket launcher and threw it on top of the fountain. Now that that disaster was out of the way, he'd take care of Richie and be on his way.

"I got him, Spider-Man!"

Spidey looked around to see a large man run out from the crowd right behind Richie. He was a real linebacker/pro wrestler type, broad shoulders, crew cut, no neck. He was probably really good at winning bar fights, but he was out of his depth here.

"No!" Spidey cried as he dashed across the plaza. "Stop it!" It was dangerous trying to take down someone desperate enough to rob a bank. Spidey had the stamina and reflexes for it, and even he got hurt sometimes. For someone who lacked Spider-Man's powers, training, and experience, a fight like this could be deadly.

But the big fellow wasn't listening. He went after Richie, both fists swinging. Richie swatted back at the big guy once, then reached into his waistband and pulled out a thirty-two-calibre pistol.

"No!" Spider-Man screamed as he leapt at Richie.

He was fast, but the bullet was faster. Richie shot straight at the large man's head.

The instant after he pulled the trigger, Spider-Man took Richie down with a punch to the jaw.

One instant too late. The big man crumpled to the ground as a dozen people screamed around him.

Somehow, the big man was still breathing. Maybe the shot hadn't hit anything vital, had just grazed him. It was hard to see exactly what damage the bullet had done; his whole forehead was covered with blood.

Spider-Man heard shouting at the edge of the crowd. He looked up to see the mob open to let through four men, two in suits, two in dark blue uniforms.

It was the police.

"Anybody see what happened here?" one of the uniformed officers asked.

"Yeah," someone in the crowd replied, "it was all Spider-Man's fault!"

What? Spidey stood up and took a step away from the fallen man's body. "Officer, these four men robbed a bank and threatened these people with guns. I stepped in here so that nobody would get hurt."

"You did a great job of that!" somebody yelled.

"Yeah," a woman at the front of the crowd agreed. "He was kidding around with these guys with guns. Somebody could have been killed!"

Other voices in the crowd joined in then:

"I thought somebody was dead!"

"What about that guy on the ground?"

The police had reached the fallen man. "Give us some

room here!" one of the officers called, pushing the crowd away.

"Is he gonna live?" someone in the crowd asked.

One of the plainclothes detectives walked toward Spider-Man. "We're going to need a statement and an explanation for all of this. I think maybe you should come downtown."

What was happening here? Spider-Man felt like he was being railroaded, charged with something he didn't do. He wasn't the guy who jumped into the fight, nor the man who pulled the trigger. He did everything he could to ensure the crowd's safety.

The crowd was yelling at him now:

"This guy's dying, Spider-Man! All he wanted to do was help!"

"It's all your fault!"

"What are you going to do about it, huh?"

Maybe they had a point. He should have checked to make sure that Richie really was down for the count. Because of that, a misguided citizen, who was trying to help Spidey, for mercy's sake, was lying there, seriously hurt.

He heard another, different siren, wailing toward them. That would be an ambulance, staffed with paramedics; one of the cops must have called it in. A trained rescue team could take better care of the fallen man than he could.

"Come on! How you gonna make it right?"

"Use your spider-powers to save him now, big shot!"

What was it I was thinking before about crowds wanting my head as much as the crooks'? he thought bitterly. In his experience, angry mobs were not the best judge of character. Maybe it was time for him to beat a hasty retreat.

"Sorry I can't stay," Spider-Man called to the detective. "I'll be in touch."

He swung to the top of the fountain, then threw the rocket launcher down to the cluster of police at the center of the onlookers.

"You can run, Spider-Man," somebody yelled from the edge of the crowd, "but you can't hide!"

Spider-Man shot out another strand of webbing and swung quickly to the low rooftop of a building across the street. Everybody was shouting behind him now, so many angry voices that he could no longer make out the words.

He thought about his camera. He'd have to retrieve it later, after the noise died down and the crowd drifted away. Maybe, considering the way things had gone, he'd quietly trash the film and forget about these pictures altogether.

He hadn't handled that situation well at all. He should have jumped in there and kayoed all four gunmen before anybody could even think of joining in. But he did a job halfway, and a man might have been mortally wounded because of that.

He swung quickly away from the scene, leaving the

crowd noise and the police sirens behind. Right now, it felt like the worst day of his life.

He heard a rumble in the clouds overhead. It was probably going to start raining.

How could it get any worse?

One

It started as soon as Peter Parker walked in the door of the *Bugle* City Room. Three different people in the space of a minute told him that the newspaper's editor-in-chief, Joe "Robbie" Robertson, wanted to see him as soon as he came in. He cut diagonally across the City Room, heading straight for Robbie's office on the other side.

The newsroom was unusually quiet today. When people saw him coming, they seemed to get awfully busy staring at the screens of their computer terminals. Betty Brant and Ben Urich still said hello, but even their greetings seemed wrong, maybe a bit too hearty, their smiles trying to cover up for the concern in their eyes. Something was going on. Every office had its share of gossip, but rumors ran wild in a newsroom. After all, as one of the old reporters had once explained to Peter, information was their business. And the news on Peter Parker that morning did not look good.

He looked up and saw Robbie's office. The door was shut; never a good sign. Peter found himself staring at the white letters painted on the frosted glass: JOE ROBERTSON, EDITOR-IN-CHIEF.

As always, there was a stack of the early edition of the *Daily Bugle* piled on the desk outside Robbie's door. Peter looked at the headline: TIMILTY VOWS TO CLEAN UP CITY!

Peter paused for an instant to glance over the front page. Anything, he supposed, to delay what was waiting in Robbie's office.

Their publisher, J. Jonah Jameson, was really pushing this Timilty character. Brian Timilty was the frontrunner in the mayoral race. He was photogenic, sort of a Robert Redford/Robert Kennedy crossbreed, and his promises and proclamations—more like rantings and ravings, as far as Peter was concerned—really sold papers. Timilty went beyond cleaning up City Hall. He had quick and easy solutions for cleaning up every corner of the city.

Maybe Peter had been in the news business for too long. No matter who got elected in New York, in a city this big the mayor could do only so much. For the most part, it would be business as usual. Most people took the subway, did their jobs, maybe caught the occasional movie or ballgame, and just got by. It was a shame so many of them still paid attention to this kind of political blowhard.

Peter was surprised by the strength of his emotions. Maybe he was still reacting to the crowd's response to Spider-Man from earlier that day. He kept thinking about the big guy with the flailing fists, and how he'd ended up on the ground, a bullet in his skull. When Peter was done talking to Robbie, he'd try to casually ask around and find out if anybody had any news about the man who was wounded.

But he was delaying the inevitable. He knocked on the door. A muffled voice said, "Come in."

As Peter entered, Robbie waved his ever-present pipe in greeting. "Ah, Peter. Good to see you, son. Why don't you close the door and have a seat?"

Peter closed the door and turned, almost tripping over the wastebasket in the corner. He had to admit, this whole thing was making him nervous.

Robbie didn't seem as comfortable as usual either. Even though he was well into his fifties, the *Bugle* editor often seemed somehow ageless, the rock that everybody at the paper could turn to for stability. Today, though, Peter could see the wrinkles etched across Robbie's deep brown forehead. Set against his full head of close-cropped white hair, for once the editor looked his age. Of course, it could just have been the aftereffects of Robbie's recent kidnapping. Along with a prominent lawyer and a police captain, Robbie had been taken and brutally interrogated by a group of terrorists only a couple of months before. As Spider-Man, Peter had aided the NYPD in rescuing them.

Still, Robbie had seemed to have recovered. And Peter suspected that his unease wasn't related to that trauma.

Peter sat as Robbie studied his pipe. The editor looked up at him at last.

"I wanted to talk to you about this personally, Peter, because it affects you more than anyone else on the staff." He sighed. "In keeping with his newfound advocacy of Brian Timilty, Jonah has made a unilateral decision. He wants to—shall we say—deemphasize super heroes in the pages of the *Daily Bugle.*"

"Deemphasize?" Peter asked. "What do you mean?"

"Timilty has been making headlines about how the media glorifies masked vigilantes." Robbie sighed. "I know you don't hound celebrities or chase down limos on a motorcycle, but right now all news photographers are being tarred with the same brush. By cutting down on certain sensational photos, Jonah feels the *Bugle* is striking a blow for responsible journalism.

"We've bought a lot of super hero photos from you, Peter. Many times, we've been able to give you special rates. But now? We can buy them from you maybe half the time, at maybe half the money.

"Here's the bottom line: No more spectacular shots of super heroes, especially Spider-Man, beating up on the bad guys unless there is a really strong story to go with it." Robbie tapped his pipe against the desk for a minute before he continued. "What this means, in dollars and cents, is that we're going to have to find you some other work. You're great at this kind of thing, and you've helped us to sell a lot of papers. Once this blows over, the same photos will help us to sell a lot more papers. But for now, cool it on the super heroes if you can."

Peter couldn't believe all this. "But how can you— Super heroes are news!"

"I know that, you know that, even Jonah knows that." Robbie paused again, considering his words carefully. "Earlier today, Jonah was talking about not using you at all anymore, as some kind of gesture of support for Timilty's campaign. You know how impulsive Jonah can be. I mentioned what a good photographer you were, how many papers you help to sell. He left talking about what a good, loyal freelancer you were."

Peter nodded. That sounded just like Jameson.

"We'll find something to keep you busy. But I wanted you to know this decision was not a reflection on your ability. It's politics." Robbie grimaced. "Specifically, Brian Timilty's politics. Whether he wins or loses, this will all die down. But in the middle of the campaign, where Jonah wants to make Timilty the people's candidate, he wants the front page to echo his editorials. Whether this will make any difference in the day-to-day operations of the paper, I don't know. But I thought you had a right to know what's going on, and I thought you deserved to hear it from me."

Peter nodded. He didn't know what else to say. Sometimes Peter thought everything at the *Bugle,* and everything in New York City, was politics.

"I'll have a new assignment for you tomorrow morning." Robbie glanced at his watch. "Now, if you'll excuse me, I have an editorial meeting in about ten minutes."

Peter thanked him and walked out the door.

He decided to get a closer look at what they were writing about this Timilty character, and so picked up one of the copies outside Robbie's office. Ben Urich had written the front-page article, which jumped to page three.

Peter whistled as he read the article. Brian Timilty—a city councillor who announced his candidacy in the spring—was out for super-hero blood. "Masked vigilantes! Agents of destruction! Running around New York, using their powers with no regard for the safety of the innocents of this fair city, attracting troublemakers from all corners of the globe. They are just as much a threat to life and property as the worst super-villain!" He singled out Punisher and Daredevil as examples of "vigilantes meting out their own brand of justice." His worst attack, though, centered on Spider-Man, who, according to Timilty, "shows an utter disregard for the law."

Wow, Peter thought. This was the "super-hero menace" that J. Jonah Jameson had written about in a hundred editorials. Apparently, Jonah had finally found his perfect candidate.

Peter closed his eyes. He had been staring at the paper the way people gaped at a traffic accident, disgusted, horrified even, but not quite able to pull himself away.

Timilty's rhetoric was full of too-simple solutions to complex problems, all reduced to sound bites. It was always easier if your problems belonged to somebody else.

There was more to the article, including rebuttals from the incumbent mayor, a "No comment" from Police Commissioner Ramos, and statements on super heroes both pro and con from various police officers who refused to be identified. Neither the Avengers nor the Fantastic Four could be reached for comment.

Maybe it's time for some dramatic photos of society luncheons. How could this day get any worse?

As if on cue, a voice bellowed out from across the City Room: "Parker!" He looked up to see J. Jonah Jameson striding toward him. *Jameson in a good mood? That's an even worse sign than Robbie closing his door.*

"It's the dawning of a whole new era, Parker," Jameson said, slapping Peter heartily on the shoulder. "Brian Timilty's the kind of man this city needs—someone who is finally going to get things done around here. With him in City Hall, all those costumed miscreants running loose in the streets will either have to clean up their acts or get out of town! The whole city will bow down and thank him when he gets rid of those vigilantes—not just the city, maybe the whole country!"

Uh-oh. When Jonah got this enthusiastic, he could talk for hours. Still, Peter couldn't help but try to inject a little reality into the conversation.

"You know," Peter said calmly, "a lot of super heroes, the Fantastic Four, the Avengers, Daredevil, they've all risked their lives to save the city from super-villains. We've run the stories in the *Bugle*. I think even Spider-Man has—"

"Spider-Man!" The very mention of Spidey's name had Jameson off and running. "I guess you didn't hear how your 'hero' almost got a decent man killed this morning! The poor man's in surgery over at Bellevue Hospital. The doctors say he's only got about a fifty-fifty chance of pulling through."

Jameson turned and banged on Robertson's door. After a moment, Robbie opened it.

"Yes, Jonah?"

"Did we have anybody to cover that robbery this morning—the one where Spider-Man went off and almost got somebody killed?"

"I got Charley Snow and Angela Yin down there as soon as we heard about it on the police radio. Charley got some eyewitness accounts, and I think Angela got a decent photo of the robbers being loaded into a wagon."

"But nothing of Spider-Man grandstanding? That's the real story! What kind of a paper are we running here?"

Peter knew he'd hate himself in the morning, but he

and Mary Jane needed the money, especially if they were going to cut his rates for super-hero shots.

"I've got shots," he said.

"What's that?" Jameson demanded.

"I shot a roll of film of the Spider-Man incident. I stumbled onto it on my way here this morning."

"Ah, Parker!" Jameson said with a wolfish grin. "Where would the *Bugle* be without you? Okay, Robbie, we're going to do an afternoon extra on this one!"

"And you're going to use Peter's photos?" Robbie asked.

"Of course!" Jameson agreed. "That's what we pay him for!"

"Including one on the front page?" Robbie prompted.

Jameson frowned. "Oh, I see what you mean. After I talked about no more super-hero photos. Well, Parker, you were in the right place at the right time. I'll pay you half rate for the front page."

"Jonah," Robbie said in a long-practiced tone of both chiding and exasperation.

"Oh, all right," Jonah said, relenting, "full rate. But don't expect me to make a habit of it!"

Jonah pulled a cigar from his shirt pocket and stuck it in the corner of his mouth. "I'm telling you, Parker, Timilty's just the kind of man we need running this city. And I'm just the man to see it happen!

"But we've got an extra to put out! I just have time to

write an editorial." He paused for a second, chewing on his unlit cigar. "How's 'So-Called Super Heroes Belong Behind Bars' sound?"

It sounded like prime J. Jonah Jameson, another chance to smear Spider-Man, with photos supplied by Spider-Man himself.

Jameson stalked off to write his editorial, and Robbie smiled at Peter, the sort of look that said, *Well, we pulled another one over on old Jonah.* Usually, this was the sort of thing that would cheer him right up.

Instead, Peter couldn't remember when he had been more depressed. Usually when he was faced by a problem too big to handle, he'd simply bring in Spider-Man. But Spider-Man was arguably the cause of both a bystander's injuries and the *Bugle*'s decision to not use super-hero photos. One reason Peter could take the time to be Spider-Man and still eat regularly was that he got those spectacular shots at the same time. Now that Spider-Man photos were mostly off-limits, how was he going to spend forty hours a week photographing flower shows and still have time to fight crime?

Peter shook his head as he walked from the newsroom. This mess was even too much for Spider-Man!

hat a dump.

Max Dillon looked out of the grimy hotel window. There was so much dirt, he sometimes had trouble telling whether it was day or night. Still, if he peered very hard, he could still read the sign through the filthy glass: THE REGAL HOTEL. That was a laugh. This place had probably been a fleabag from the day it was built.

He looked around the tiny room, painted institutional green, complete with cracked plaster and a sagging bed. The only royalty that might have stayed here was the king of the gutter.

He looked across the room and saw half a dozen small brown creatures skittering over the far wall. It figured. Usually, roaches stayed out of the way of bright lights and people. These suckers acted like they didn't care. They peeked out from behind the faded landscapes hanging on the wall, danced across the bathroom sink, died in the overhead light fixture. There were so many cockroaches in this place, the Regal Hotel could probably advertise them as in-room entertainment.

They were fast little buggers, too, zipping from one hiding place to another with lightning speed.

Fast as they were, though, Max Dillon was faster.

He picked one of the half dozen at random, pointed his index finger at the scurrying bug, and sent out a jolt of pure electricity from his fingertip. The cockroach jerked a couple of times, its legs spasming in a final wild dance as it fried. The blackened carcass dropped to the worn, brown carpet.

The electric charge had left a tiny burn mark on the wall. Not that anybody would notice that sort of thing in a place like this.

Dillon went back to the bottle he'd been emptying for a good part of the evening, then decided to burn half a dozen more of his scurrying roommates. It helped to pass the time. Hell, he was providing a service for the Regal here—Max Dillon, exterminator! They should pay him for staying in this crummy hotel.

Once, Dillon had been a lineman for the power company. A simple, dreary life that had been the result of a simple, dreary childhood. That all changed when a lightning bolt struck him while he was up on the pole. It should have crispy-fried him—instead, it turned him into Electro, the master of electricity. He fashioned himself a costume and proceeded to strike terror into the hearts of people everywhere.

At least, that was the idea. Someone always stopped him—usually Spider-Man.

So when the Rose—what a stupid name for a criminal mastermind!—came to him and offered to increase Electro's power a hundredfold, bring him right up there with the power elite like Magneto and Dr. Doom, of course Dillon said yes.

But even with that kind of power, the Rose had lost. So had Electro.

The power elite. The words made Dillon want to laugh all over again. All those guys, they were always trying to take over New York City on their way to taking over the world. Over the past couple of years, locked in a prison cell, Electro had watched both Magneto and Doom try again to own the world, and he watched them fail. And he had figured out exactly where they, and all the other masterminds before them, had gone wrong.

All of them had called too much attention to themselves, made themselves the enemies of super heroes everywhere, made themselves too public and too vulnerable. Electro had a better way. Why take over the world when you can just take all the world's money instead?

Ever since that last mess with the Rose, Max had decided to keep it simple. He would work with a few chosen people, nobody too high profile, and stay completely behind the scenes until the moment he was ready to act. No world domination for him. Just manageable crimes, like blackmail, extortion, industrial espionage, and maybe a little low-risk theft.

Electro would never do what they expected. He would never be caught again. He knew what worked for him. Better living through electricity. He'd get the rest of New York to see that too, then just take the money and go.

A knock came from the door. "Boss," came the muffled voice of Dillon's new employee. "You ready?"

Dillon smiled. Davis was early. He admired that.

He fried another cockroach for luck, then got up to let Davis in. It was time to go to work.

Peter Parker had found out the name of the man who had jumped into the fight—John Garcia. He had been rushed to Bellevue Hospital, as Jonah had said, where they immediately operated to remove the bullet from his skull. The operation had been a success, and despite what Jonah had told Peter back in the newsroom, the doctors were "cautiously optimistic" about his recovery—whatever that meant, especially since, after the operation, Garcia had lapsed into a coma.

Peter decided he wanted to pay this Garcia fellow a visit. He felt like he'd spent too much time lost in thought. It was time to go out and do something. It might not make any sense, but he knew he would feel better if he could see

Garcia in person, watch him breathing, see with his own two eyes that the wounded man had a chance.

Not that Peter Parker would have any chance of getting near him. While Garcia was in a coma, they'd placed him in the Intensive Care Unit, and were allowing only family members to visit. Members of the press were being ushered into a small room in the hospital's basement, where, every four hours or so, they would be given an "informational update" where a hospital spokesperson would tell them there was no new information.

Spider-Man, however, could crawl wherever he wanted, including into third-floor hospital windows. Visiting hours would be over by now, and even the ICU should be fairly quiet. He swung quickly from skyscraper to skyscraper through the dark Manhattan evening, intent on doing this one last thing before he went home to Mary Jane.

His wife always helped him gain perspective when he felt like he was in over his head. *Boy, do I need to talk to Mary Jane tonight.*

The warning jolt from his spider-sense was so sudden, his stream of webbing completely missed a windowsill. He swung to the nearest wall and hung there for a moment, waiting for some sound or movement to go with the warning.

Instead, there was light. A blinding flash came from one of the windows beneath him. He swung his body around to get a better look. Another flash, not quite so bright as the first, came from a window only two stories below him. Lights appeared to be flickering on and off in the room below. He crawled quickly toward the window. As he approached, he became aware of a faint but constant noise, sort of a humming noise with an occasional static crackle, like the sound of a power-station generator.

One wouldn't usually expect to find a generator in an upper-story midtown office, unless, of course, the generator had walked in there on his own two feet. Spidey knew of only one person who had that kind of fun with electricity.

Heads up, Electro, Spider-Man thought. *It's time to stop the light show.*

First he looked for a place to set up his camera. Sure, they didn't want as many super-hero snapshots, but that didn't mean no pictures. Besides, fancy pics of Spidey fighting Electro, the air alive with electricity, Electro's power meeting Spidey's webbing midair, that wasn't just a news photo, that was art! He set up his camera, hanging from a web line, at the very center of the window. That would give it a clear view of the action.

He crawled down to one side of the window. It was an old building, one where the windows actually opened and closed; most modern skyscrapers had sealed windows, particularly in a city where people who could fly or walk on walls were so prevalent. The lighted window was open just a crack.

Spidey pushed it all the way open and slipped silently inside.

This, "Fast Anthony" Davis thought, *is a lot like the Fourth of July.*

Electro had brought him along to the Office of Water and Power to find some "important information." Once Davis had jimmied the locks, he found himself standing around as his boss used his power to quickly check through computer files and apparently burn a few computer terminals along the way. Davis wasn't sure if he was here to watch Electro's back or serve as Electro's audience. What was the difference, anyway? Davis had learned to step back and let Electro do his thing.

Davis had to admit that Electro wasn't always the most coherent of bosses. All that electricity had probably done something to his brain. But hey, Davis didn't have to get up in the morning, the hours were short, and the job promised to make him rich beyond his wildest dreams. He could put up with a little craziness for that.

Something—a shadow, a noise, a movement—caught the corner of his eye and made Davis turn around.

Spider-Man was crawling through the window.

There was no time to pull a gun. There was no time to do anything but shout.

"Boss! Behind you!"

Electro turned as Spidey leapt across the room. Electro ducked from the attack, but Spider-Man's boot caught his shoulder, causing the electric man to stagger back into a file cabinet.

Davis wondered if he could get a clear shot at the web-slinger, but the other two were moving so quickly, he was afraid he might shoot his boss or some piece of equipment that held the information Electro was looking for. He thought it best, for the moment at least, to step back from the action.

"Here, Electro," Spidey said, "a little present." He sent a mass of webbing sailing toward Davis's boss, but Electro replied with a quick bolt of electricity. The crackling line of power met the descending webbing in midair, causing the web to fry instantly.

"What?" Spider-Man called. "I'm beginning to think you don't want to celebrate."

Davis sidled over to the window, thinking if there was a roof nearby, it might be a safer place to be. There wasn't even a ledge, but there was something on the other side of the glass. A camera, right in the middle of the window, hanging from a single strand of webbing.

Webbing? Was Spider-Man taking pictures of himself? What was he doing, planning to advertise?

Davis looked back to the action. Electro shot twin charges of power out from his palms, straight at Spider-Man. Except the hero was already gone. The twin arcs of current smashed into a pair of computers against the far wall. Both monitors exploded with a great flash of light.

"Pretty spectacular," Spider-Man agreed. "Tell me, do you know all the words to 'You Light Up My Life'?"

But Davis couldn't stop thinking about the camera. This could go beyond Electro. Fast Anthony Davis had to look out for himself, after all. Maybe, if he could grab the camera, he could find something he could use. It might even have something about Spider-Man's secret identity or something.

Davis jumped back as a bolt of lightning shattered the glass.

Electro laughed. "All I have to do is connect once, Spider-Man, and you're done for."

"There's a phrase for guys like you, Electro," Spider-Man called back as he dodged around the room, looking, no doubt, for an opening to get at his opponent. "I think it's *power-mad*. Tell me, did you have pictures of Speedy Kilowatt in your room as a—"

The hero barely dodged a bolt of power. Something exploded behind him. Spider-Man was showered with broken glass.

Spider-Man was literally bouncing off the walls as Electro sent bursts of energy to every corner of the room.

Davis dove under the nearest table.

"That smarts! What's your friendly neighborhood Spider-Man ever done to—"

He heard Spider-Man yelp in surprise, followed by a tremendous crash. Electro had finally gotten in a good shot.

Davis peeked out of his hiding place. Spider-Man had been pushed back through not one but two sets of plaster walls. He lay there in the rubble, three rooms away, barely moving.

Davis stood up and walked over to his boss. "Maybe you should finish him off."

Electro shook his head. "Spider-Man can wait. Let's get what we came here for." He turned and stared at the devastation around him. "All the computers are smashed! Spider-Man made me destroy the files!" He looked up at Davis. "Maybe I will kill him after all."

Both of them looked back to the rubble. Spider-Man was nowhere to be seen.

"Wow," Davis whispered. "How could he get back up after being pushed through two walls?"

"Maybe he's crawled off to die," Electro suggested.

"Either that," Davis replied, "or he's getting set to ambush us again."

They stood there for a very quiet moment. Far too quiet after the mayhem that had just passed.

"There's nothing here you need, right, boss?" Davis asked.

Electro nodded. "I say we get out of here."

Davis was very glad to hear that.

It was only when they were halfway down the fire stairs that Davis remembered the camera.

Oh well, he thought, *it was probably a long shot anyway.*

* * *

They were gone. Electro and the young black man in the mirrorshades had left the room, without whatever they had been looking for.

Spider-Man lowered himself gingerly from where he'd plastered himself up against the ceiling. Only after he'd confronted Electro had he realized how unprepared he had been for the fight.

Electro was still the same souped-up version Spider-Man had faced a couple of months back—far stronger than he used to be. Spidey landed as gently as he could on a clear spot in the midst of the rubble, testing his arms, legs, and neck. Remarkably, nothing felt broken. He might have slightly twisted an ankle, and he certainly bruised his ribs. He was just grateful his ruse worked, and Electro hadn't come looking for him. Even with his remarkable recuperative powers, Spider-Man imagined he was going to be sore for a couple of days.

After that, all he had to figure out was how to beat a villain with enough power to light up New York City.

Who said his life wasn't starting to look up?

Three

The Rhino was tired.

It had started two weeks before. The tenement he had been living in felt too small, the walls of his room closing in on his massive seven-foot, five-hundred-pound frame. But the streets had given him no peace. Even without his armor, people shuddered when they saw him. They wouldn't look him in the eye, walked to the other side of the street, sometimes even lifted their arms in front of their faces, as if he were going to hit them. He had had too much of his dead-end life.

Still, he walked down the streets at the lower end of Manhattan, day and night, through rain and sunshine. He had no idea where he was going, but he knew what he was searching for. He had been looking for a way out.

And there, two weeks ago, in the middle of the street before him, had sat the armored truck with a flat tire.

He had acted on instinct then, like the poor dumb animal that was his namesake. A truck like that meant money for the taking, money to get him out of this pit of a city, out to somewhere where he could start a real life.

He'd heard of a place in Florida, a whole town filled with carnival performers who had retired or just lived there in the off-season. They'd even based an episode of *The X-Files* on it, a place where even somebody as big as the Rhino wouldn't be treated like a freak, where maybe little old ladies would smile as he passed instead of cowering at his size, a place where he could just lead a normal life.

He wanted peace. He wanted security. He'd seen the armored car, with the two guards turned away, and he had snapped.

He had rushed the truck, shouting at the top of his lungs, a shout that would scare anybody. He didn't have his armored suit to protect him, but he was as fast as his animal namesake, too, knocking out both the guards before they could fumble for their guns.

The whole thing was a mistake. Not that he still couldn't rip the door off the back of an armored truck without breaking a sweat. But he should have had more of a plan, waited for a more secluded location for the robbery. If he was going back to crime, he should have done it with some style.

But he didn't, and he paid. As soon as he had reached

the truck, who should swoop out of the sky but Spider-Man. He was in the middle of Manhattan—Spider-Man's turf. What had he been thinking?

They had fought all too briefly. Spider-Man had defeated him all too easily. The Rhino knew why. He had only been half-trying. He really didn't want to steal anymore. He just wanted to get away, and needed the money to do so. He wanted peace and security. He just wanted to get away.

Next thing he knew, the cops had him in a titanium steel cage that even he couldn't break. So here he was, in a special cell again, trapped here day after day. Two whole weeks! It felt like forever.

He wasn't supposed to be here even two days. It seemed like the red tape was getting worse and worse, even in prison. So he was stuck cooling his heels at Ryker's Island Penitentiary while they pushed through his transfer to the Vault, the Colorado facility for incarcerating superpowered criminals.

So he sat in his cage and waited. Mostly, the guards around here just left him alone. They probably knew when a con just didn't care anymore.

He looked up. Someone was banging on the bars.

"Okay, Rhino, your transfer came through."

They always did these transfers first thing in the morning. Probably didn't disturb the rest of the prison population or something if they got people out of there before breakfast. Rhino stood, his head brushing the top of his special cell. He'd never escape from the Vault, but it would be better than this cage. They would give him a room large enough to move around in, a place to exercise, things to keep him busy. When your life was made up of being taken from one prison to another, you learned to appreciate the little things.

He stood patiently while he was fitted with titanium cuffs and leg irons. A pair of guards led him from the cell-block and out to the courtyard. There, sitting in the early-morning light, was a small police van, its lights still on—the van that would take him to the airport and a special plane, which would in turn take him to the Vault.

There wasn't much in the way of security out here: a pair of guards, a pair of cops, and a single gate between him and the freedom of the outside world. There were probably a couple of guards with guns in the tower over-head. Rhino thought for an instant about making a break for it, but discarded the idea. He was fast, he was strong, and he might be lucky enough to dodge most of the bullets. But where would he go once he was out? He was too big to hide. Without money or other resources, they'd simply track him down and put him away for even longer.

"Okay," one of the guards said. "We got your prisoner." He sounded bored.

The cops opened the back door of the van that was going to start him on his way. It was smaller than the ve-hicles they usually used to cart him around, but it looked brand new. Probably made of some high-tech, superstrong alloys, guaranteed Rhino-proof. He looked into the dark interior. He hated enclosed spaces. The back of the van looked barely big enough to hold him.

One of the cops laughed. "What's the matter, buddy, don't want to take the scenic tour?"

The Rhino thought briefly about slugging him one, but this whole thing was his own fault. If he hadn't gone off half-cocked after that armored car, he wouldn't be here today. Better to just get this over with. The Vault kept most of the super-powered cons separated from each other. A lot of the time, it felt like you were in solitary confinement. Right now, Rhino was looking forward to at least that version of peace and quiet. He crawled into the back.

The compact police van could barely hold his bulky frame. The walls were a shiny white, with two strips of light on either side of the ceiling. A single bench ran along the compartment's left-hand side. He had to hunch forward even when he was seated on the bench.

They slammed the door. Usually, they bolted his leg chains to the floor while one of the cops rode shotgun in the back, just out of his reach. This van wasn't big enough for that.

There was actually a small window in the back of the van. Probably some modern plastic as strong as the steel around it. But it actually gave him a view. He couldn't see where he was going, but he could get a look at where he had been.

He watched as the cops signed a couple of forms on the

clipboard and walked out of his sight. He heard them climb into the front of the van.

They started the engine.

"Next stop, La Guardia," a voice said from above his head. Must be a hidden speaker somewhere. "Sit back, Rhino, and enjoy the ride."

Then they were moving. Rhino saw the prison gate close behind him.

"So, Rhino," the hidden voice continued, "want to answer some questions to pass the time?"

Rhino didn't feel like talking. He especially didn't want to listen to annoying questions.

"How tough are you, really?" the voice went on. "Think you'd like a chance to show us?" Two voices laughed.

Great. The cops, protected by some high-tech barrier, were going to make fun of him. The Rhino knew what to do with people who mocked him. He looked at the featureless white walls around him and wondered how reinforced the steel of this van really was. Many people underestimated the Rhino's strength. The next time the cop started joking, he could punch his fist through the sheet metal and choke him.

No, Rhino thought again, it was because he was ticked off, because he was feeling trapped, that's what got him here in the first place. There had to be another way.

He had to be kidding himself. Another way to do anything, once he was stuck back inside the Vault?

Once he'd been arrested, he had stopped fighting. In the outside world, there had been too many options, all of them just out of reach. Now there was only one option. He might not want to go there, but at least he had a place to go.

The van stopped. He hadn't looked out the back window for close to ten minutes. Even from half a dozen feet away, he could see movement outside. Where the hell were they? He pushed himself down to the end of the bench to get a better look.

They were supposed to be on their way to La Guardia. They should be driving down some backstreet in Queens, full of row houses or squat brick warehouses. Instead, he saw tall buildings to either side, with people pushing racks of suits and dresses back and forth across the street. Rhino recognized the neighborhood. They were stuck in the stop-and-go traffic of lower Manhattan.

He banged on the side of the van. "This isn't the way to the airport!"

"Who said anything about the airport?" the disembodied voice replied. "I told you we were taking you on the scenic tour."

Rhino felt the anger bubble up inside him again. "What kind of cops are you?"

He was answered by laughter.

"Who said we were cops?"

"We work for somebody bigger than the police," a second voice chimed in, "somebody that wanted to do you a favor."

"A favor?" This was crazy. But why else would they have driven into Manhattan? "You mean he's springing me? I'm free?"

More laughter. "Nothing's ever free. You gotta go see our boss."

Rhino banged his fist against the partition between him and the drivers. He put the slightest of dents in the metal. And he hurt his hand.

"You ain't goin' anywhere," the voice advised him. "Sit back and enjoy the ride."

Tyler Stewart put down the phone. *Sometimes,* he thought, *life just can't get any better.*

What had that *Daily Bugle* article called him last week? "Mr. Money." That was it. The new player in town, with a dozen apartment buildings and office towers already to his credit, and maybe, if a certain new mayor got into office, a new convention center to add to the mix.

He looked again at the color photo that had led off the *Bugle*'s Living section. His full, neatly trimmed beard, the still-dark hair, with only a trace of gray despite being well into his forties, the square shoulders, the direct blue-eyed gaze. He was the very picture of success.

The newspaper piece had been a hoot: Tyler Stewart, brilliant businessman, upstanding citizen. The *Bugle* had no idea where most of his money really came from. When you played this big, everything looked legitimate.

A little money stuffed in a pocket here, a death threat or

two there—it was a wonder how much the proper combination of graft and fear could get you. Tyler Stewart, good for business, bringing a new, more prosperous future to New York.

Of course, there were some folks in the underworld who weren't as trusting as his friends on the newspaper. They knew where the real deals were. And they also knew Stewart's weaknesses.

But Stewart had come too far to fall now. He had decided he needed a little extra protection, someone to watch his back once the other bosses realized how powerful he'd become.

Someone like the Rhino.

Stewart always thought that the simplest plans were the best. Corruption was everywhere, if you knew where to look for it. It had been the simplest of tasks to slip the forged transfer papers for the Rhino into the system. Then all he had to do was repaint his largest armored van and bribe somebody down at the uniform supply house to lend them a couple of blues for the day. And bingo! One large, homicidal maniac indebted to Tyler Stewart. And Stewart intended that the Rhino would pay that debt in full. How, he wasn't quite sure yet. But he knew something would come up.

But he had other business to attend to, even on a quiet evening in his town house. His butler had let him know that Michael Luce was waiting in the living room. Luce was the best political consultant money could buy, so Stewart had bought him. Brian Timilty's campaign was going exactly as planned. Then, with his own man in office, Stewart could *really* get to work.

People didn't know parts of Luce's past either, like his early career as an assistant to Silvio "Silvermane" Manfredi, former leader of the New York branch of the Maggia crime syndicate. When Silvermane had gone down, Stewart had convinced Luce that his devious brain might be put to even better use behind the scenes, and the former gangster had found his true calling as a political consultant. Stewart liked working with a man like Luce. They both knew too much about the other to ever go public.

Stewart greeted Luce as he entered the room.

The consultant turned away from where he had been staring at the roaring fire. Stewart had had the ornate brick fireplace imported whole from a fourteenth-century castle in Scotland. It was an impressive sight.

Luce hadn't changed in the ten years they had known each other. A decade younger than Stewart, Luce was still rail thin and kept his long, straight hair tied back in a ponytail. Although only in his early thirties, Luce somehow gave the impression of an overage hippie in a business suit.

Luce greeted him with a big grin.

"Spider-Man," was the first word out of his mouth.

Stewart laughed. "Could the timing be any better? That scene at the bank robbery plays right into our hands."

Luce paused and scratched at his right temple. "You know, this could be the beginning of a trend. I can see the headline: ARE SUPER HEROES DANGEROUS TO YOUR HEALTH? Maybe we could create a few more 'accidents' and really get the public aroused. What if the Thing were to toss some creeps around Yancy Street, say, and someone gets buried in the rubble?"

"Brilliant." Stewart really liked the way Luce's mind worked. "But I think we should concentrate on Spider-Man first. He's already given us an opening with the by-stander at the bank robbery. What if we can show him being careless again, maybe even putting a whole group of citizens in danger?"

"I like it," Luce agreed. "Give me a little time, and I'll come up with something to trash Spider-Man for good. It's a great idea, Stew. We'll play up the 'ban super heroes' angle of Timilty's campaign, and Spider-Man can be our poster boy."

Both of them had a good laugh at that. Stewart clapped Luce on the back. "Ah, Michael. What can I say but 'Do your worst'?"

Michael Luce found himself almost giddy with excitement.

His life was a lot like the glass elevator he rode in now, from Stewart's penthouse to the lobby. He could see all of New York spread out before him on one side, a twenty-story atrium in the building's center on the other, but he saw it all from a glass cage. He had power and money, all the trappings of success, but he felt cornered by the life he'd chosen. He could have almost anything in the world, but was hemmed in by convention. These days especially, politicians—and their consultants—had to keep up appearances.

He could still remember when he ran on the other side of the street, working behind the scenes for Silvermane. He was young, and he felt like there were no limits. Oh sure, looking back on it now, he probably romanticized the excitement and minimized the very real danger in which he often found himself. But he rarely felt anything like that excitement now.

That's why he valued his relationship with Stewart so highly. Luce had mostly left the criminal world behind, but Stewart kept one leg firmly in the underworld. He had a paid killer on his security staff. And he had plans that, once Timilty was elected, would make them all rich beyond their wildest dreams.

Most candidates had scruples; they would let Luce go only so far. With Stewart, there were no such limits. Luce found it very refreshing.

It was side projects like this that kept him alive. By the time he was done, Spider-Man wouldn't just be finished, he would be dead and buried.

Luce stepped out onto the street and turned toward Fifth Avenue.

Another figure stepped from the shadows across the street. Luce had spent close to an hour in the building's pent-

house, clearly seen going up and down in a glass-walled elevator.

And now? Michael Luce, Timilty's campaign manager,
and the most highly paid political consultant on the scene
today, was seen coming out of Stewart's penthouse in the
early evening, when the streets were full of commuters,
when anyone could notice, when anyone could make the
connection.

Clearly, some things had to change.

The shadow figure would follow Luce for now. Maybe
the consultant would reveal a few more secrets, show how
the pieces fit among Luce and Stewart and Timilty and
who knew who else?

The figure could wait for just a little while longer. But
soon the puzzle that was Luce and Stewart and Timilty
would be smashed for good.

Four

Fast Anthony Davis didn't see the photo at first. It was hidden on the corner of page five, not plastered all over the front page like most photos of Spider-Man. Davis wondered why they'd bury a photo like that. Wasn't Electro news?

It was only then that it hit him; this picture came from the camera hanging outside the window. The photo credit read P. PARKER—DAILY BUGLE. But there had been no one up anywhere near that room. *Spider-Man must have some sweetheart deal with this Parker, where Parker gets the credit for the photos and Spidey gets publicity to stroke his super ego. Wow. That mayoral candidate—what was his name? Timothy? Something like that. Anyway, what that Timothy was saying about super heroes just being in it for themselves, it's really true. And this proves it.*

This, Davis decided, had to be worth some money. Not to Electro, though. He was too busy with his big plan, not that he'd ever bother to completely describe it to Davis. No, Davis needed someone who bought and sold information, who could figure out the true value of something like this.

Davis called a man he knew. Yeah, he had something he thought they would find interesting. No, he didn't want to talk about it over the phone. He was still home in Brooklyn now; how long would it take him to get over to Tyler Stewart's headquarters?

No more than an hour.

Davis hadn't seen Andy for close to two years, but the other man hadn't changed. His round, pale face under a mass of dark curls looked disarmingly innocent. He always dressed dramatically, today wearing a pinstriped jacket and ruffled shirt. He always stood out, even appearing a little foppish. Davis always figured he was looking for someone to make a crack about him so that he could turn around and kill them. Murder, after all, was what Andy lived for.

Andy went by only the single name. When Davis had done the occasional job for Stewart in the past, he'd asked some of the regular gang members why. According to Tom "Fingers" Devlin, who generally drove for most of Stewart's jobs, rumor had it that, as a child, Andy dropped his last name right after he murdered his parents.

For a couple of years, Davis had helped out on the occasional job for Stewart—an arson here, a breaking and entering there. He'd even made a couple of suggestions to improve Stewart's organization on the street level. But then, for some reason, the calls from Stewart's associates had stopped coming. Davis wondered if the big boss was getting too legitimate, and didn't want to associate with someone who had come up off the streets. Davis had always done what was asked of him, and Stewart had always paid off on time. But the jobs didn't increase over time. He didn't think he'd done anything for Stewart in over a year and a half.

Of course, once he'd hooked up with Electro he'd had steady work again, and enough money to get by. But Stewart was a whole different ballpark. Electro was working on one big score. Stewart was probably working on hundreds.

Electro's job was almost done. In a couple of weeks, Davis might be looking for work. If this information gave him an in with Stewart's gang, so much the better.

"Andy," Davis said as they approached each other in the lobby of Stewart's headquarters.

Andy giggled. He never shook hands. Generally, he kept one of his hands in a pocket, curled around a knife.

"Let's go someplace private," Andy said very softly.

Davis followed Andy back to a small office behind the elevators. Andy sat behind a beaten-up old metal desk. He waved for Davis to take the chair on the other side.

"So when do I get to see Stewart?" Davis asked.

Andy reached into his pocket and pulled out a switch-blade. He pressed a button on the side and a four-inch blade popped out. He looked up at Davis.

"Nobody sees Mr. Stewart directly. A lot of people are trying to get a piece of Mr. Stewart's action. You have a history with us. Otherwise I would have just hung up the phone." He tapped the knife against the metal desk. "So what have you got?"

Davis tried to figure out the best way to put this. He wanted Stewart to remember him, to think about him next time he had a little work. He needed to give just enough so that he'd be taken to the boss, but not so much that Andy could relay the information for him.

"Well, Andy, I found out something about Spider-Man."

"Really?" Andy looked up from where he had started to stab the knife into a worn blotter. "You may be in luck. Spider-Man is very big upstairs these days." He paused and looked straight at Davis for the first time. The gaze felt so intense, Davis half expected it would bore straight through his skull. He glanced away.

"You know, of course," Andy added softly, "that noth-ing goes beyond these walls."

It was the usual understanding. One word about his as-sociation with Stewart, and he was dead. For Andy, killing stoolies was a hobby. Davis looked back to the other man and nodded once.

Andy smiled. "Actually, there's another reason you're here. Are you still tight with Electro?"

Davis was a little surprised that Andy knew. He and Electro had been trying to keep everything low profile. Or at least they had until that fight with Spider-Man.

"I do work for him every day," he replied. It was a little bit of an exaggeration. Electro didn't seem able to get it together every day. But they'd been working on this new plan off and on for the better part of a month.

Andy giggled. "Then you have two reasons to see Mr. Stewart." He stood. "Come on with me."

He pulled a drawer out on one side of the desk. On the other side of the room, a file cabinet rolled silently aside to reveal another elevator. "The private way," Andy said. "We're taking you right to the boss."

Now, this, Davis thought, *is class.*

The elevator they rode up in was small but wood-paneled. Dark stuff, too—cherry, maybe. Andy rode up beside Davis. He'd put his switchblade back in his pocket, where he also kept his right hand. Didn't want to scratch the wood by accident, Davis guessed. Andy said nothing as the elevator climbed, but he giggled twice.

The elevator opened to a wall of glass. Beyond, he could see the Empire State Building and Central Park. Even the thick gray carpet beneath their feet screamed money.

This, Davis thought, *is where I need to be.*

Andy led the way to a set of large wooden doors, also cherry, to the right of the elevator. "The boss is in through here."

Andy opened the door and they walked through to the other side. Davis stepped into a huge office with another panoramic view of the city. Tyler Stewart turned from where he had been staring out the window.

It was interesting, seeing Stewart again after a couple of years had passed. While physically he looked much the same—the beard, the wild mane of hair, the square shoulders and burly chest, all somehow imprisoned inside a tailored business suit—Stewart seemed far quieter and more assured than he had the last time Davis had seen him.

"Welcome, Mr. Davis." He strode quickly across the carpet to meet Davis and Andy midroom. "These are my personal offices, where I conduct only my most private business." He smiled ruefully. "I don't think you've seen this place before."

Davis shook his head. "You were still finishing the building the last time—"

Stewart slapped Davis on the shoulder before he could finish. "I realize that we haven't been able to contract your services much of late." Stewart paused, watching Davis for a long moment. "However, I believe we may be able to use you more often in the future."

That was just what Davis wanted to hear.

Stewart directed him to one of two overstuffed chairs

that looked out over the city. When they were both settled, he nodded. "So tell me what brings you here."

Davis quickly described his discovery of the camera, and the photo that had appeared the following day.

"Really?" Stewart cupped his hands together and nodded. "I may know some people who can use that information in the near future. You might be able to help us there."

He looked up at Andy, who hovered by the arm of his chair, then back at Davis. "Would you care for anything? I have a fully stocked bar."

Davis shook his head. He was too nervous. If alcohol got involved, he'd either spill it all over himself or drink too much and make a fool of himself. "No, thanks."

Stewart nodded in return. "Then I have only one other question for you. Could you possibly set up a meeting for us with this Electro?"

Davis didn't answer at first; he was too surprised. Stewart wanted to meet with Max Dillon? Why?

"I guess so," Davis agreed. "Electro's going to want to know the reason for the meeting, though."

"I would expect no less," Stewart agreed. "It's for a business deal of sorts, which I believe he will find very much to his advantage. Tell him that I guarantee that he won't be disappointed."

Davis considered this. It still seemed pretty vague. "You couldn't give me one or two specifics that I could dangle in front of him? Electro's been an independent operator for most of his career. Whenever he's worked with someone else, it's always turned out badly. He just might need a little persuasion."

"A good point," Stewart agreed. "Why don't you convey our sympathy to your employer about the lack of results from your visit to the Department of Water and Power? I may be able to help him gather the information he needs." He glanced out the window, then looked back to his guest. "If Electro agrees to meet with me, I'll give him a special bonus." The businessman grinned. "Spider-Man on a platter."

That, Davis thought, *might just do the trick.*

Five

Peter Parker had no doubt had worse photo assignments, but right this minute he couldn't think of any.

Robbie Robertson had, as promised, called him with his first new assignment that morning: to come in at ten A.M. to take some shots of their publisher with Brian Timilty, candidate for mayor. The *Bugle* was doing a week-long set of interviews with the various candidates, trying to get their views on a number of local issues. Today was Timilty's turn, and to top it off, Jonah, in a rare move, was doing the interview himself. Jonah usually confined his writing chores to his publisher's editorials.

"You can do wonders with costumed guys in motion," Robbie had told him over the phone. "Now, here's a real challenge—make two talking heads look interesting."

Thanks a lot, Robbie, Peter had thought as he put down

the phone. Given Timilty's views on Spider-Man—and Jonah's—he expected the encounter to be infuriating, to say the least.

He wasn't disappointed.

Peter had shown up at 10:02. His publisher had been standing in his office with two other men, all three talking intently about "the modern voter" or some such. J. Jonah Jameson looked over as Peter entered.

"Parker. About time. Meet the next mayor of New York." He waved at Timilty.

So much for impartial reportage, Peter thought.

"And his campaign manager, Michael Luce."

Timilty nodded to Peter. "Michael makes sure my tie's on straight and I don't have ketchup on my chin." The candidate did have a disarming smile. He was, if anything, even better looking than those campaign posters that were plastered over every inch of free space downtown. What was the slogan? "Timilty—For a Better Tomorrow."

Michael Luce, on the other hand, was totally unremarkable. Scrawny, with his long hair pulled back in a ponytail, he was the sort of person you'd pass on the street without looking twice. He certainly didn't look like the country's most successful political consultant, with over a ninety-percent success rate in getting his candidates elected. Until this moment, Peter had never seen a photo of the consultant. Luce was something of a mystery figure, managing to keep himself out of the spotlight almost as successfully as he placed his political clients center stage.

The fact that Timilty could afford someone like Luce meant that he had some real money behind him, although the candidate had so far avoided revealing exactly where this war chest had come from.

Peter told both of the men he was pleased to meet them. He decided to try to sneak Luce into a few of the shots so that maybe the *Bugle* could share his likeness with the readers as well. Sort of a very quiet scoop, the kind of thing that kept a job like this interesting.

"Shall we start?" Jonah's voice brought Peter back from his thoughts. "Brian, if you'll sit here," he indicated one of two comfortable chairs the publisher had installed in one corner of his office, "and I sit over here, there should be plenty of opportunity for Parker to get some good shots." He sat in the opposite chair. "Now, where would you like to begin?"

Timilty talked about why he wanted to be mayor in the first place, how we was looking for "a return to basic values." Peter noticed he didn't give any indication of what those values might be.

Instead of picking up on the point, Jonah waxed nostalgic about the good old days of New York, when all they had to deal with was old-fashioned street crime.

Peter was doing his best to ignore the exchange, trying to get the publisher and the candidate smiling, frowning, making an angry point, a dramatic hand gesture, anything that would make this fairly static meeting look dynamic on the printed page. He took a few wide-angle shots that included the two, and a couple of arty shots over one speaker's shoulder with the lens focused on the other.

Getting Michael Luce in the camera frame was another matter entirely. If Peter hadn't been looking, he might not have noticed the way Luce skulked around the room at all. On a few occasions, especially when he was using the wide-angle lens, he had tried to catch the political consultant reacting to the two men talking. Michael Luce moved quietly around the periphery of the conversation, always keeping just out of Peter's—and the camera's—way. Peter turned quickly at two different occasions to shoot a candid of the consultant, but Luce was faster. One time Luce turned away; the other he had a hand in front of his face. *No wonder I've never seen a photo,* Peter thought. Luce obviously guarded his privacy.

Peter turned his attention back to the interview. Timilty was going on at some length about super heroes.

"One sort breeds the other. If we are ever going to control the super-powered men and women who want to damage our fair city, we need also to control those self-proclaimed vigilantes who protect our city, or so they say. It is my contention that without super heroes, there would be no super-villains."

Jonah sneered at that. "Not that you can tell the difference between them sometimes."

"Sometimes," Timilty agreed, "I don't think there is a difference." He leaned forward in his seat. "Have you noticed, since the arrival of super heroes on the scene in New

York City, violence has been steadily on the rise? These sort of larger-than-life characters inspire that sort of reaction. In a way, they demand it. And it will only get worse. At the very least, they'll have the whole city living in fear of their actions. If their power remains unchecked, they could destroy the world."

"I've been saying that in my editorials for years!" Jonah waved one of his fists in the air. "I'm glad we finally have a politician who has the guts to tell it like it is!"

Peter was losing it. They were blaming super heroes for every negative thing that had happened in this city for the last decade. He felt his hands shaking as he held the camera. He had to say something.

"Wait a sec." He looked at Jonah. "Are you saying that because Daredevil or Spider-Man stops a mugging, the city is going to fall apart or the world is going to end?"

Jonah frowned. "Parker! You're here to take the pictures, not ask—"

"No, no," Timilty interrupted. "Peter here has a good point. No one is saying that the super heroes haven't done some good in this city. Heaven knows they take a bite out of street crime. But our problem is that they're unregulated. They take it upon themselves to change the city in whatever manner they feel best, without the input of any outside authority. New York already has one of the finest police forces in the world, made up of people whose backgrounds are thoroughly checked before the first day they take the safety of the city into their hands. Aside from rare exceptions such as the Avengers, the same cannot be said for super heroes."

Peter couldn't believe what he was hearing. "But super heroes have saved this city a thousand times."

"But at what cost?" Timilty asked. "Look, for example, at how much property they destroy in those super-powered fights of theirs. And that is far from the worst of it. Just look at the incident over at the Mid-Pacific Bank the other day. Spider-Man and his ilk are endangering the life of every citizen in New York City."

"My point exactly!" Jonah cheered.

Timilty nodded. "I'm surprised that sort of accident doesn't occur more often. If indeed it was an accident. Doesn't someone like Spider-Man, with his lawless behavior, encourage the sort of mob violence that left this poor citizen—" He paused.

Luce materialized at the side of his chair. "John Garcia," the consultant prompted.

"Garcia, right, a man who only wanted to help, but was cut down in the prime of his life."

"Cut down?" Peter had had just about enough from this windbag. "Garcia isn't dead."

Timilty smiled condescendingly as he shook his head. "He's in a life-threatening coma. Isn't that just as bad? Perhaps, if he's lucky enough to pull through, we as a city may be able to learn this lesson without losing a life. The likes of Spider-Man must be controlled, or they should be taken off the streets forever."

The logic of all this was completely backward. "You talk about super heroes being unregulated. But what gives you the right—"

Timilty suddenly got to his feet. "I have the right because I have the vision. I will be the next mayor of New York City!" His tone, which had been modulated and reasonable until now, was tinged with anger. He looked like he was ready to throw a punch Peter's way.

Peter realized that he had let the situation get out of hand. The only responsible thing to do was to get out of here.

But Timilty wasn't about to let him go. "Who are you? A news photographer? What do you do besides point your camera and shoot? You haven't studied this city the way I have. You have no idea how complex—"

Michael Luce stepped in between the two of them. "Brian, please. This guy isn't worth it."

Peter was speechless. This was the second situation he'd been in in two days that had totally gone out of control. At least this one didn't involve rocket launchers.

Jonah looked up at him. "Don't you have enough photos, Parker?"

Peter nodded. He had taken close to four rolls.

"Well," Jonah continued, "in that case, I think it's time you got those developed." He waved Timilty back to his seat. "We can conduct the rest of our interview in peace. Parker, shut the door behind you. And I'll want a word with you later."

Peter did just that.

He hadn't meant to get that angry. But how could Timilty take one isolated incident like what happened outside the bank and blow it way out of proportion?

Peter took a deep breath. Timilty could do it because he was a politician, and it was easier pointing the finger at super heroes than debating who would get less money, fat-cat developers or homeless children.

Once the adrenaline wore off, Peter realized all the things he should have said, instead of provoking Timilty. He should have pointed out that many super heroes' backgrounds were well known. The Fantastic Four's lives were an open book, and as Timilty himself admitted, the Avengers all had to go through government clearance. And they cooperated with the authorities. Daredevil, Spider-Man, the New Warriors—they, too, had worked with conventional authorities on more than one occasion. And the NYPD was not equipped to deal with the likes of Venom or Dr. Doom or the Hobgoblin.

But Timilty would probably repeat his line about how there would be no super-villains without super heroes.

He had been hoping his initial feelings about Timilty were wrong, but, if anything, his first impressions had been too kind. If Timilty got into office, Peter felt the next four years would be a living hell, not just for Spider-Man, but for every super hero in New York.

Sighing, Peter put the four rolls he'd shot into an envelope, then walked the twelve steps to the newsroom so he could drop them off on the photo editor's desk for processing.

The first regular assignment, and he'd almost gotten into a fistfight. What next? He could see it all now: PHOTOGRAPHER BRAINS SOCIETY MATRONS WITH PUNCH BOWL! STORY ON PAGE 3! And on top of everything else, he was going to receive one of Jonah's patented tongue-lashings, which tended to be loud, irritating, and long.

He should be fair to himself. This whole thing started when John Garcia tried to help Spider-Man out and got shot for his trouble. Peter had been feeling guilty about it ever since. What, short of Garcia's full recovery, would make Peter feel any better?

"Hey! Is that the best news photographer in New York City?"

Peter looked up. Perhaps there was some hope for today after all. There was a vision of loveliness walking toward him across the City Room. More specifically, it was his own personal vision of loveliness, Mary Jane Watson-Parker.

She gave him her fabulous Mary Jane smile, known far and wide from her modeling gigs and her stint on a soap opera. She looked just moderately gorgeous today in jeans and a green sweater that brought out the green in her eyes and complemented her long, straight flaming red hair. "Hi, handsome. Going my way?"

"Every moment of every day," Peter agreed. Maybe this day wouldn't be a total washout after all.

"My class got out early." MJ had been taking psychology courses at Empire State University. Sometimes, between her psychology homework and his double life, they hardly saw each other. "I thought you might like to get some lunch?"

Peter grinned at her. "Breakfast, lunch, dinner. I'm available. Right now, all I want to do is get out of here."

She offered him her arm. Right this moment, he felt like the luckiest photographer in the world. He'd have to tell MJ about all of his problems over lunch. Somehow, she'd see a way out of it.

"Well, if it isn't New York's premier couple!" Ace reporter and very old friend Betty Brant got up from her desk and came over to say hello. Betty was probably the first real friend Peter had had on the *Bugle*. They had even dated for a while when she was still J. Jonah Jameson's secretary. Now, though, with her fashionably cut dark hair and understated business suit, she looked the part of one of the *Bugle*'s star reporters. With all the changes Peter and Betty had been through together, they both still felt a strong connection. Whenever something went wrong for Peter at the *Bugle,* she was always there to lend a sympathetic ear.

"That was quite a fight in Jonah's office," she said with a smile.

Peter winced. "You heard that?"

"The entire office did. We decided you were winning until the TKO."

"TKO?" MJ asked.

"Jonah tossed him out of his office," Betty said with a smile.

MJ glanced at Peter. "Oh, are *we* going to have some things to talk about at lunch."

Peter shook his head. "If I don't just start ranting about Timilty. I'm beginning to think he's as bad as the Friends of Humanity," he said, referring to the grassroots mutant-hating organization. "I see the same holier-than-thou attitude coming out of Timilty, except this time he's got it in for all super heroes, not just mutants."

Betty gave them both a knowing smile. "Well, you might find that Timilty isn't quite as holy as you might imagine."

"Sounds like Betty's got a story," MJ observed as she squeezed Peter's hand.

Betty hesitated for a moment before continuing. "I'll give you guys something else to chew over." She glanced around the newsroom to make sure that no one else was nearby. "An exclusive."

She lowered her voice to little more than a whisper. "I decided to follow our Mr. Luce, and found him coming out of Tyler Stewart's penthouse."

"Really? I think we might be seeing the source of Timilty's bottomless campaign fund."

"And a sweetheart deal," Betty agreed, "that will probably greatly benefit Stewart once Timilty is elected. I think the whole lot of them are crooked, and as soon as I can check some facts, I intend to blow the whistle on them."

Peter whistled softly. "Wow. If you can show that Timilty is in Tyler Stewart's pocket, suddenly the golden reform candidate doesn't look so golden anymore. I think most of the city would agree that they wouldn't want to elect the puppet of 'Mr. Money.' This whole anti–super-hero campaign would pop like an overheated balloon."

Betty studied Peter for an instant, a small frown line creasing her forehead. "You seem to be awfully keen on this anti–super hero business, Peter."

"And why wouldn't he be?" Mary Jane jumped in. "Usually, taking pictures of super heroes is his bread and butter."

"Plus, I just can't stand Timilty's hypocrisy," Peter agreed, glad for MJ's quick thinking.

"Well," Betty said, "once I check a couple of my facts, you may not have to worry about his hypocrisy anymore."

"But Jameson seems pretty hot on this Timilty character," MJ pointed out. "Will he really print the story?"

"Once I get all my facts in place, and present a firm case? Jonah will have to go with it then. It's news."

Peter agreed with Betty. No matter what Jameson's opinions, he never censored the truth. That was why, despite his opinions, J. Jonah Jameson published the best paper in town.

Betty excused herself, saying she'd better get back to work.

"I think it's time to get out of this place and find some lunch," Peter said.

Peter squeezed MJ's arm. Maybe things would start looking up after all.

Six

Electro was not in the best of moods.

At first, he hadn't even wanted to listen to Fast Anthony. But Davis had persisted, telling his boss that this meeting could make his task much simpler. Stewart had connections. Anything Electro wanted to know about the Water and Power Authority would be his in a matter of hours. Besides which, they'd throw Spider-Man into the bargain!

Electro sighed. When he no longer had to be grateful to the Rose for the increase in his power, he had thought he finally had it made. Great power and no obligations; with a combination like that, he could go wherever he wanted. And, while doing a little research at the New York Public Library—all right, he had had Fast Anthony do most of it; too many books gave Max Dillon a headache—he had figured out a way for it all to come true, a way to bring New York City to its knees, and make him rich in the bargain.

It had seemed so simple then. He had the theory in place, but he needed exact facts and figures for it all to come true. That was what their little visit to the Municipal Power and Water Authority had been about. But then Spider-Man had shown up before Electro could even find the proper file!

His plan was brilliant, but he wanted to keep it close to his electrified chest. He didn't want to give away too much too soon. Even someone clever like Fast Anthony might have been able to pull off this sort of job without him. It was just that being a human dynamo made a big project like this so much easier.

Now he was going to have to share something of his plans with a man who built skyscrapers and had politicians in his pocket; a man who had the resources to make anything happen. Electro still didn't want to share a thing. Oh, maybe a little bit of the money for Davis, but Fast Anthony was a product of the streets. He could be bought off easily, or even disposed of without anybody paying any attention. Stewart was another matter entirely.

Still, Electro had certain advantages. One well-placed million-volt shock, and Stewart was as dead as the next man. Electro wanted it all. He was tired of these would-be power brokers using him. This time, Electro would use Stewart instead.

Davis was still waiting for him back in the car. Well, when did Electro ever need anybody else? They had been met in the parking lot by a burly, slightly overdressed fellow whom Davis referred to as Andy. Andy had giggled when introduced, then told Electro to follow him.

It was an odd place to meet. Electro wondered if Stewart liked to inconvenience people to make himself feel more powerful. The place was now called the Queens Theater, stuck right in the middle of Flushing Meadow Park, but Electro remembered it as the home of the New York World's Fair in the early sixties. He remembered his fascination for the pavilions that dealt with the future of electricity, nuclear power, and even fossil fuels and natural gas. He smiled. They had called the last one "The Festival of Gas." Nineteen sixty-four had been a whole different world, a world before the accident that made Electro what he was today, a world before there was even a Spider-Man.

That, Electro knew, was the real reason he was here. This might be a convenient way to get the information he needed, even if there would be bills to pay, obligations to fulfill. There were other ways to get what he needed, but the chance to finish Spider-Man, the hero who had stopped him time and again and kept Electro from fulfilling his destiny—that was what Electro couldn't refuse.

Somehow, Spider-Man had always interfered with his plans, always defeated him when he could almost taste the victory. Electro supposed he had become a bit superstitious about it. Even something as foolproof as his current scheme would probably fail somehow because of Spider-Man.

Ah, but if he could get Spider-Man out of the way forever? That was something that he was willing to pay for, one last time. With Spider-Man gone, nothing could stop him.

The pavilions of the World's Fair were long gone, but a few of the structures remained. First and foremost was the Unisphere, the great wire-mesh globe that was the centerpiece of a fountain, spewing water even this late at night. To the left of the giant globe was what looked like a gutted amphitheater—the Queens Theater. To one side of the structure were a pair of towers topped by large disks, looking like nothing so much as a pair of plates. He was reminded of the old Ed Sullivan show, where performers would balance a dozen plates on the end of a dozen poles. The towers looked just like that.

When they had first constructed all this for the World's Fair, it had seemed like a sign from the future. Now the buildings all looked like big clunky objects from the early sixties. How much had changed in thirty-odd years. It was fitting, though, that they were meeting so close to the giant world. Soon, after all, the world would be his.

They left the Unisphere and the twin plates behind, and walked into the open-air Queens Theater.

"The new theater's over there," Andy explained as they passed through the open gate and started down the ramp that led into the open amphitheater. "Our business is in here, the old theater. They call it the Arena." Then he giggled again.

Three men stood in the middle of the open circle of the Arena, two toward the center of the circle, the third well behind the others. He recognized "Mr. Money's" broad shoulders and beard from all the way across the Arena. Tyler Stewart's face graced as many magazine covers these days as Donald Trump's or Tony Stark's. America loved money. But who was Electro to criticize? He loved money, too.

Only one light burned in the place, a floodlight that illuminated the front of the stage where Stewart stood with one of his cronies, a tall, thin man who fidgeted constantly, as if he had trouble standing still. The other man remained well back in the shadows but stood out, even in the semi-dark. He was massive. Electro wondered what there was about him that seemed familiar. Maybe Electro had seen the big man when he was a football player or a professional wrestler.

"Ah. Electro," Stewart said as they were halfway down to the stage. "We are honored you could join us."

Honored? Electro still didn't like this. He could fry any of them as easily as he did those cockroaches back in his hotel room.

"Excuse the out-of-the-way meeting place," Stewart continued, "but this corner of Queens doesn't get used much this time of night. And I'm rather fond of the architecture. You saw the Unisphere outside? Coming here when I was a boy, the very bigness of this place made me want to build things."

So the World's Fair had inspired Stewart as well. Electro was surprised to find that the two of them had something in common. Then again, lots of people were impressed by the Fair.

"But the real reason we're in Queens in the middle of the night? I thought we could use a little privacy." Stewart waved up at the great disks at the back of the theater. "In a way, this place is as big as our dreams, eh?"

Electro stopped as he reached one edge of the large circular space in the center of the theater. Andy continued on to join his boss.

"And we want to help you fulfill your dreams, Electro. I understand you want some information about the Department of Water and Power? I happen to have informants in that very department. Not surprising, really. I have informants everywhere. The first rule for success: Know what your competition is doing. The second rule? Know what everybody else is doing, too." Stewart laughed like this was some sort of joke. Andy giggled along with him.

"But you need access to that information." He snapped his fingers. "Devlin?"

The thin man stepped forward, walking across the arena to Electro.

"My man is going to hand you a slip of paper," Stewart explained. "On that paper is the name and number of the man at Water and Power who will give you whatever you need to know. Simply identify yourself as Max Dillon—that is your proper name, yes?—and this individual will give you anything you need."

Devlin approached Electro very cautiously. He handed Electro the paper as if he half expected the man to burn him with his touch. A little fear always made Electro feel better. He looked down at the paper in his hands. On it was scrawled the name David Kornfeld and a 718 phone number.

"Then the—ahem—power is in your hands, isn't it?" Stewart said from where he still stood in the middle of the circle. "If there's anything else you need, please don't hesitate to ask. Not that I need to know what all this is for. If we're going to be friends, we need to learn to trust each other."

Sure, trust. Electro almost felt like laughing. That's why he had a thug hanging back in the shadows, and probably another guy or two covering them with guns. Not that any of them could stop Electro.

"So what do you want from me in return?"

"Oh, nothing much. Just your guarantee that you'll help me on a project of my own in the near future. This could be the beginning of a very profitable association. You've got power, Electro. I've got cash. Together, they would make a great combination."

They still hadn't gotten around to discussing one of his main reasons for coming. "Davis mentioned something about Spider-Man," Electro prompted.

"Oh yes," Stewart agreed. "That should be one of our main goals of working together. Rest assured, my friend, that sooner or later we will eliminate Spider-Man."

Andy giggled again, as if the thought of a dead Spider-Man was highly amusing. Electro would laugh only after Spider-Man was dead.

Stewart waved to the thin man, who still stood close to Electro. "Our man here is Tom Devlin. 'Fingers' to his friends."

Devlin held up a hand in greeting.

"He will be your contact," Stewart continued. "Fingers is very resourceful."

"Then we're done here?" Electro asked.

"For tonight. I look forward to a long and profitable association."

Maybe, Electro thought. It hadn't cost him anything so far.

Somehow, that made him even more suspicious.

Davis quickly turned from where he had been watching at the top of the theater. He needed to get back to the car before Electro and Stewart discovered he was spying on them.

It had taken him all of about two minutes, sitting there in the parking lot, before he decided to follow Andy and his boss to their meeting with Stewart. There was no way he was going to sit in that Lincoln while the two men he brought together had their big powwow. He was in Electro's employ, and he wanted to get back on the good side of Stewart. How could he do anything for anybody unless he had all the facts?

No. That's what he'd tell them if they caught him following them. But he was extra cautious. Andy was good at catching furtive movement and sounds that didn't belong, so Davis hung way back as Electro and Andy marched across the grass, walking across the beginning of the park only when the others had passed the Unisphere, and hiding out of sight behind the fountain until he was sure which building they were going into.

The Arena seemed like the perfect place for Stewart. He liked things big.

Davis trotted back to the car before Electro could even turn to leave. He was quite pleased with the results. They would all be working together after all. That could only be good for Davis. The more Electro and Stewart succeeded, the better for him. He had been a little worried about putting two egos like that together, but it seemed to be working out fine.

Of course, sooner or later, maybe after Electro's project was complete, or maybe even after they'd killed Spider-Man, the two of them would argue. Maybe one would even kill the other.

No matter who came out on top, though, Fast Anthony would be the winner.

Seven

Brian Timilty could feel it. He was going to win it all.

Here it was, close to midnight, and he couldn't stop pacing around his living room. He didn't feel the least bit tired. The latest pay-per-view action flick on his fifty-inch television couldn't hold his attention. He had to be out in public bright and early the next morning. Luce had planned a full day of appearances and sound bites for him. He really should get some rest.

But how could he rest when he had the whole city in his hands? Just look at the newspapers! And not only that puff piece in the *Daily Bugle*. There were news stories and op-ed pieces in every paper in town, from the three major dailies down to the low-circulation free weeklies. All of them quoted the more-than-encouraging polls. Luce had been correct. Find someone to blame for all the city's ills, someone like the super heroes. Go for the throat and the public will come along to watch the blood.

Timilty sighed. He really shouldn't have let the photographer get to him today. Malcontents like Peter Parker were the exception, not the rule. When he was mayor, he could ignore those do-gooders and get on with the business of running the city his way.

But the whole city was going his way already. There were three other pieces in the *Bugle* alone that said even more than his interview. One story described how Daredevil was attacked by an angry mob when he tried to apprehend a purse snatcher. Another reported that the New Warriors were actually pelted by garbage when they showed up in one of the more colorful sections of Brooklyn. And then there was Jameson's latest editorial: "Bring Down the Vigilantes." For someone so easily led, Jameson was one heck of an editorial writer. The way he exhorted the citizens of New York to take back their city from those costumed clowns—hell, he even had Timilty believing it.

And then, of course, there were the poll results, twelve points ahead of the incumbent mayor, three points ahead of where he was the week before and climbing. How had Luce phrased it? *Give them fear, give them anger, and the voters will come.*

Now, Timilty thought, was the time to stay the course, and perhaps exercise a little caution. Perhaps, at least until after the election, he might even slightly distance himself from Stewart. He would be more than happy to throw his political weight behind the moneyman's future projects, but that was after he was elected, when he could talk about doing it "for the good of New York." Best not to appear to be too deep in Stewart's pocket. A last-minute scandal had brought down bigger politicians than Timilty.

The phone was ringing. He picked up the receiver. It was Luce.

"Stewart needs to see you right now."

"At this hour?"

"It's best to meet at odd times," Luce replied calmly. "That way, we have less chance of prying eyes. By now, all the reporters are either safe in bed or hanging out at their favorite bars."

"But—"

"He *is* the moneyman. He made it all possible. Even with all the new money coming in, we could use his help on the last-minute media blitz."

"Okay," Timilty said. Luce told him he'd have a car out front in ten minutes.

This, he realized, showed how much he trusted his campaign manager. No matter how crazy any of this had sounded at first, Luce had never steered him wrong. Timilty had gone from a first-term city councillor to the leading contender for mayor, thanks mostly to a cleverly orchestrated photo campaign and the "Take Back New York from the Super Heroes" business.

Why did Stewart need to see him now, in the middle of the night?

He hoped it wasn't a money problem. The last week's radio blitz was sure to cement the campaign.

Maybe they needed to have their own little talk with Stewart. This would be as good a time as any. Surely Stewart would see the wisdom of distancing himself from the campaign in the final days before the election. Timilty sometimes had difficulty talking to the man, but his campaign manager and the builder went way back. He was sure Luce could get him to see reason.

He looked out the window. A long, black stretch limo waited for him down on the street.

Timilty grabbed a topcoat from the closet and hurried down the stairs to meet it. Luce usually picked him up in his Mercedes. They used a limo only for formal functions. Maybe his campaign manager's car was in the shop.

He quickly set the burglar alarm and locked the front door. He turned and looked at the car below, but hesitated at the top of the steps to his brownstone. There was something about an all-black stretch limo sitting in a deserted street in the middle of the night that seemed a little sinister.

Timilty took the first three steps down toward the street, then paused again. What if someone besides Luce was waiting for him in the car?

A window at the back of the limo rolled down. Michael Luce stuck his head out.

"Get in, Brian."

The door opened.

Brian went down the rest of the steps and stuck his head inside the car.

His campaign manager was not alone. Tyler Stewart sat across from him. Next to Stewart was another man, stockily built, wearing a Hawaiian shirt with colors that seemed to glow even in the soft illumination of the limo's overhead light.

"This is Andy," Stewart explained. "I only bring him when things are getting serious. Brian, get in the car."

Timilty looked to his campaign manager. Luce nodded. So he did as he was told, shutting the door behind him.

Stewart rapped on the glass behind him, glass that separated the passenger compartment from the driver. The limo started to move.

Stewart smiled. "We thought it was time for our little talk, now, before you got into office. And you will get into office. We've seen to that, Brian."

This, Timilty thought, *is all very strange.* Still, considering where he was in the polls, he could afford to be magnanimous. "Well, Tyler, you've been very generous toward my campaign. Your money saw us over a lot of rough spots, especially early on, and I want you to know that I'm grateful—"

"Money? This is about far more than money. The money is just the icing on the cake, isn't it, Andy?"

The man next to Stewart giggled. He seemed to be fondling something in his shirt pocket.

Stewart beamed at his associate as a father might smile

at a favorite son. "There was no cause for you to meet Andy before now." He looked at the two men in the opposite seat. "Perhaps there will be no need for you to ever see Andy again."

Michael Luce cleared his throat. "Stew, don't you think you're being a little heavy-handed?"

"Shut up, Michael. What I'm being now is clear. I've paid for something with more than just money, and now I'm planning to collect."

This was going too fast for Timilty. Perhaps he was more tired than he realized. "What do you mean, you've paid in more than money?"

"I've done you a few favors," Stewart replied. "True, you didn't specifically ask me for any of them, but without them, you wouldn't be in the advantageous position you are today."

He didn't like the way this was going. "Favors?"

"Well, there was that ex-wife of yours," Stewart allowed.

"Gloria? You've done something to Gloria?"

Luce shifted in his seat. "I had something to do with that, Brian. Even though the two of you have been divorced for more than two years—"

"And a messy divorce it was," Stewart added.

Luce glanced over at the moneyman in annoyance. "Well, yes. But we discovered that, even though all legal ties were separated, Gloria would periodically come to you looking for money."

Well, that was true. Gloria never could quite get her life in order. But that was no reason for them to interfere. Their marriage didn't work out on mutual grounds. Timilty was really married to his career, while Gloria seemed married to spending all of Timilty's money. Still, they had shared a short time together.

"If you've done something to Gloria . . ."

"Only gotten her out of the way," Luce assured him.

"She works for me now," Stewart added. "Cushy job. She hardly even has to show up at the office. That way, she's a lot less tempted to sell any information to the tabloids. And we can keep an eye on her besides."

Timilty thought about it for a moment. When Gloria ran out of money, which she often did, she could get a little desperate. Giving her something to do until the election was probably a very wise move. But he had never told anyone, even his campaign manager, about his problems with his ex-wife.

He looked across at Stewart. "How much do you really know about me?"

"It's my job to know," Stewart replied. "About you, and everything else that happens in my city."

Andy looked to his boss, a shy smile on his face. Very softly, he said, "Tell them about the rest."

Stewart nodded. "There have been other favors. Some even our Mr. Luce doesn't know about."

Michael looked uncomfortable.

"What?" Timilty demanded.

"Well," Stewart replied, "there was that scandal involving the Reverend Peterson."

That was their doing? Until that scandal broke, Peterson had been his strongest challenger in the primary election.

"Such a shame, really," Stewart continued. "But a man of the cloth having a relationship with a married woman, well, even the citizens of New York could only take so much."

Andy giggled.

"It was our civic duty to announce it to the press," Stewart added, "after, of course, we had introduced the Reverend to Mrs. Murphy and gave it a few weeks to heat up."

"It was very thoughtless of Mrs. Murphy," Andy added softly, "to neglect to tell the Reverend about her husband."

"And it was tragic about the accident that killed Councillor O'Meara's wife." Stewart's expression said that it wasn't tragic at all. "Rumor has it the accident caused him to withdraw from the race."

"Tragic," Andy agreed. He giggled.

"We knew you didn't want to dirty your hands, but someone had to. We've done a few more of these little favors. We'll list them if you really want to know."

Luce shook his head. "I don't."

Timilty was speechless. So they'd gotten rid of his strongest competition through dirty tricks? It sounded like they had bolstered his campaign through bribery, scandal, maybe even murder.

"Why did you do this for me?" he asked instead.

"You don't have any scruples. Just a politician's ego and a lust for power. You were perfect." Stewart patted Timilty's knee. "And because you're perfect, I will give you power. And you, in return, will give me everything I want. I have plans for Brian Timilty."

"Look here, Stew," Luce objected.

"Shut up, Michael."

Andy giggled.

But Timilty wanted to hear what his campaign manager had to say. "Michael?"

Luce shrugged. "Well, when Stew really gets something in his head . . ."

Stewart nodded. "People used to die. That doesn't happen so much anymore. I'm above that sort of thing. I have other people do it for me."

Andy giggled again.

Timilty still couldn't accept this. "But we never agreed to any of this."

"The minute you started taking my money, you agreed to everything. You've now got a debt that you'll have to pay off with the rest of your career." It was Stewart's turn to laugh. "Oh, I'm not so arrogant to think we can do these things right out in the open. We will always have a very good reason for any favor you do for me, a reason that seems to help the city. And we'll see to it that you'll do plenty to make sure you're the hero of the people, including driving every single super hero from New York." He clapped his hands. "How about this? No one can have a fistfight over Manhattan without a permit. They'll all have to move to Cleveland. And we'll have an even freer hand to pursue the important things."

"Important things?" Timilty asked.

"Subverting the permit process, bribing building inspectors. I've already got my own people in most of the different departments around the city. You'll get a list so that you can help us promote from within. We're going to make Manhattan Mr. Money's town!"

Timilty was appalled. This was the man he was going to talk into backing down? He obviously didn't know Stewart at all. "And I'm supposed to stand by while you take over the entire city?"

"No, you'll be busy making headlines, just like you're doing today. You'll be the hero of the people, driving out Silvermane, Hammerhead, the Rose, Fortunato, all the warring crime bosses that give the city a bad name. Because, from here on in, there's only going to be one boss in New York City—Tyler Stewart.

"I've been doing this for twenty years. An article last week named me as almost single-handedly responsible for pulling the city out of a financial crisis or two. That may be a bit of an exaggeration, but I won't complain. For the last two years, I've been big enough to make and break financial crises, and I've done it when the situation called for it.

"I already own New York, Brian," Stewart said. "You're just going to make it official."

No. This is all wrong. Timilty had made compromises to get where he was, but if he caved in to this maniac, he'd lose his last shred of self-respect, his last iota of decency.

He stared hard at Stewart. "I'm not going to jeopardize my election, no matter what Michael Luce has told you."

"Whoa!" Luce threw up his hands. "I've got no part in this. I guess part of me always knew he'd want more. But I've done my best to put my criminal past behind me. Stew here still wants to wallow in his."

Stewart smiled at this. "Everybody needs a hobby, Michael."

As usual, Andy giggled.

Timilty looked at Luce. "You have a criminal past?"

Stewart was clearly enjoying himself. "You didn't know he used to work for Silvermane? Oh, he's dirty, Brian. I'm dirty, too. And now you're as dirty as the rest of us."

"But—" Timilty began again.

Stewart cut him off. "Enough. It's late. I am very disappointed with the both of you."

Timilty noticed that Andy now had a switchblade in his hand. He smiled benignly at the two men across the way as he flicked the blade in and out, in and out.

"You either work for us or you don't work at all," Stewart said firmly. "It would be a shame if you couldn't fulfill your duties as mayor. I'd have to come up with a brand-new candidate for the next election." He shook his head.

"I'd be slowed down a little. For me, it's inconvenience. For you, we're talking about your life."

"Brian," Luce said, "I'm afraid you're going to have to listen to him."

"All right," Timilty admitted. "Perhaps we could come to some understanding." He was suddenly very tired. "Do you think you could take me back to my townhouse now?"

"Oh, you're not going anywhere until I'm done, either of you. I think it's time I showed you who has the real power around here." He looked back and forth from Luce to Timilty. "Not, of course, that I'd dirty my hands, even with you. But then, what do I pay the likes of Tom Devlin and Andy for, anyways?"

He paused a minute before he added, "You two are going to go for a little ride."

This was like some bad gangster movie. "A ride?" Timilty asked.

Stewart laughed. "I suppose that does sound a bit melodramatic. No, we're not talking cement overshoes, at least we're not if you cooperate. Andy hasn't killed anyone in a very long time. No, I'm sending you out to bring me someone else.

"Tonight, you are no longer the next mayor of New York and his top political consultant. Tonight, gentlemen, you are bait."

Andy giggled.

Eight

Nobody wanted to see Spider-Man tonight.

That business at the bank had been all over the papers. And that story, along with Timilty's campaign, and J. Jonah Jameson's editorials, seemed to be influencing opinions everywhere.

His usual evening patrol of the city had seemed to produce one disaster after another. One of the mugging victims he'd saved in Greenwich Village acted like he expected Spider-Man to mug him instead. A woman had actually screamed when he'd swung overhead near Times Square. And when he landed between two rival gangs to prevent a potential shootout in Chinatown, the gangs and the onlookers had all turned on Spidey, yelling at him to go and leave them alone. These were tense times for a super hero, especially one by the name of Spider-Man.

On top of that, Electro seemed to have disappeared. Maybe the villain was just lying low, but Spider-Man was sure he disrupted some small part of something big. The most Electro could hope to gain from invading a municipal office was information, certainly part of a much larger plan. And once Electro got started on one of his schemes, Spider-Man knew he would continue unless he was stopped.

Spidey decided to take one final circuit of the outskirts of Central Park. There weren't many people out at this time of night, even in New York. Swinging high above the empty streets was one of the ways he could sometimes find peace. If everything was quiet, he'd be better served to cut his losses, go home, and get some sleep.

He felt the slightest tingling of his spider-sense as he heard voices raised below. It sounded like two men, shouting back and forth. Could it be a fight? It was somewhere nearby, just around the corner. He swung around the side of the building to get a closer look.

It seemed like a normal argument, except that he recognized the two men arguing from when he had met them earlier that day—Michael Luce and Brian Timilty. What were the next mayor and his top consultant doing out at this time of night? *Inquiring minds want to know,* Spidey thought. He'd hang around for a minute and see what was happening.

They were walking toward a limousine. There was nothing strange in the late hour, or that they continued to yell at each other. What was strange was a third man who walked behind them, a heavyset fellow in a bright Hawaiian shirt with an old-fashioned, broad-brimmed hat pulled low over his face. Both Luce and Timilty were aware of him. Each would steal glances back at the third man as the two continued to fight. The man with the hat, on the other hand, didn't say anything.

Spidey was close enough now to pick up some of the words.

"And your criminal past!" Timilty was shouting. "How convenient that you forgot to tell me about that!"

"My past has never interfered with my job before," Luce shot back, much calmer than his boss. "You went into this with your eyes open. I warned you when we first started taking money from him that he could be difficult."

"Difficult? A man who threatens your life is a lot more than just difficult!"

By now, they had made it down to the end of the sidewalk. The man walking behind them motioned for them to get into the car. When he waved his hand, Spidey saw the glint of metal in his hand, reflected by the streetlights.

That's what his spider-sense was trying to tell him. The third man had a gun.

The two others didn't seem to notice. Their argument got even louder.

"There's always a certain amount of risk," Luce insisted.

Timilty laughed harshly. "Risk I can handle. Compromise is a fact of politics. I scratch your back, you scratch mine. It's the sort of thing that keeps a city like New York running. But this isn't anything like compromise." He turned to glare at the man with the hat. "This is more like kidnapping."

The third man lifted the gun so that both men could easily see it.

Luce shook his head. "You know," he said in a quieter tone, "that's what is weird about this whole thing. A part of me admires it. This is like the old Stew. Anything goes."

"It's all just politics, huh?" Timilty replied, a certain resignation in his voice. "I just never expected it to be quite this *cutthroat.*"

Luce shook his head. "You get what you pay for, huh?"

Both of them actually laughed at that, though Timilty's laughter sounded nervous.

"You know," Timilty said as he opened the door. "I don't know if my life's in danger, or if this is just a game."

The man with the hat spoke for the first time, his voice much softer than either of the others. "With my boss, sometimes it can be both."

Luce shrugged. "You wanted cutthroat, you got cut-throat."

Timilty shook his head. "I just never imagined it was my throat getting cut."

The hatted man waved them toward the car one more time. "Gentlemen?"

Timilty threw up his hands in defeat. "Okay, Andy, we're going."

"This sort of thing could definitely interfere with the campaign," Luce warned the third man. "I don't approve of this arrangement."

The man named Andy actually giggled. "This isn't the end of it by any means. Oh no. This is far from over."

All three of them got in the back of the limousine. The car pulled away. That meant there were at least two others in the car with Timilty and Luce—Andy and a driver.

So the man who wanted to outlaw super heroes, and the media man who was making his campaign possible, were both being held at gunpoint. What was a super hero to do?

Spider-Man decided he'd better follow the limo. Maybe there'd be some way to save them.

Not that he expected them to thank him. But stranger things had happened, just in the last twenty-four hours. Maybe Spidey could turn this whole thing around.

Timilty couldn't believe this.

He was supposed to be the next mayor of New York City. Except that he was really supposed to be the puppet of Tyler Stewart and his underworld connections. Unless, of course, Stewart decided he wanted Timilty dead.

None of this made sense. If Stewart was so keen on using Timilty as his front, how could he throw him away? If Timilty was going to make Tyler Stewart the true power in New York City, how could Stewart's hired gun be about to shoot them?

Andy sat across from Timilty and Luce in the limousine, fondling his gun. He began to sing softly—so softly that Timilty couldn't make out the lyrics. Even before he started singing, Luce had convinced Timilty that Andy was capable of anything.

From Stewart's actions, Timilty wondered if the same couldn't be said of Andy's boss.

Stewart had left them after his initial threat. He'd told Andy to keep in touch by phone and tell him of their "progress," whatever that meant. This was the third time they had stopped. Each time Andy told Timilty and Luce it was time to take a walk. He would call Stewart when they left the car, and call him again when they came back. Then they would drive someplace else, seemingly at random.

The first time they had gotten out of the car, neither Luce nor Timilty had wanted to do much but stand around in sullen silence.

"No, no," Andy had instructed. "You need to walk and talk. Mr. Stewart's orders."

"What do you mean?" Timilty had demanded. "Why do we have to—"

"You walk and talk, or I shoot you," Andy replied in that same quiet voice. "Only a flesh wound this time. But it'll hurt, and it will simply ruin the line of your coat." A high giggle bubbled from the back of his throat.

So much for arguments. Timilty tried to think of something to say. Luce talked about the Jets' chances in the coming year. Timilty had always been a Giants fan.

Still, they managed to talk about something for that trip out of the car, and the next one, too. But Andy was always with them—Andy and his gun. The tension had to go someplace. By the third time out of the car, they were openly arguing with each other.

"That was good out there this time," Andy said after they were all safely back in the car. "Raised voices are sure to attract attention."

What? They wanted to draw attention to two men being pushed around by a gunman? Timilty and Luce looked at each other, but neither spoke. By now, they knew that Andy didn't like answering questions, and he carried a thirty-two pistol and a switchblade to make his point.

Andy picked up the phone and punched a single button, speed-dialing to Stewart. "Third location complete," he said after a moment. "Instructions?"

He nodded and put down the phone.

"Stewart wants you to be careful."

Timilty couldn't help himself. "Careful? Careful of what?"

Andy stared at them silently a moment before speaking.

"He wouldn't have you doing this unless it were absolutely necessary."

It was in those rare moments when Andy was serious that he was truly frightening. Timilty still wanted to ask him more. He nervously ran his thumb across the ripped upholstery between his legs, a reminder of what Andy had done the last time he had talked too long.

Stewart's hired gun had already turned away. Andy stared through the roof's one-way glass. His giggle turned to an outright laugh.

Andy quickly placed another call to Stewart.

"The spider's on the web."

He looked at Timilty and giggled again.

"Now we only have to drive one more place."

Timilty looked at Luce in the silence that followed.

"Then what?" he asked at last.

"Then we wait."

Timilty frowned. "Wait for what?"

"You'll see." Andy giggled.

It was almost too easy for Spider-Man to keep up with the limousine. It averaged twenty to twenty-five miles an hour through the nearly deserted Manhattan streets.

The limo didn't go in a straight line. It zigzagged across town, even backtracking a couple of blocks at one point. Apparently, they were wary of being followed. Too bad they didn't look overhead to see they were being accompanied by a friendly neighborhood Spider-Man.

The limo eventually pulled up outside of a warehouse

a stone's throw away from the West Side Highway. The driver got out of the car and spoke into an intercom. The loading dock door opened noisily, and the limo drove inside.

Home at last, Spidey thought. Now he just had to find his own way into the warehouse.

His spider-sense started tingling as soon as he landed on the top of the warehouse. Spidey looked around, but all was still and silent. The roof appeared to be deserted. The spider-sense must be warning him about something inside. Spidey scratched at his chin. He could have guessed it was dangerous in there without all this tingling.

He found a stairwell with an unlocked door at the far corner of the roof. *Pretty careless of the security staff.* He guessed they weren't expecting any Spider-Men.

Silently, he crawled downward along the stairwell.

The second floor of the warehouse had flooring only around the edges, and that was mostly full of large boxes stamped PRODUCT OF HONG KONG. This was an import-export place, pretty typical of this part of the city. Spidey wondered what was really in these boxes.

Not that he had any time to check just now. The center of the second floor was nothing but naked girders, with a clear drop to the warehouse floor some twenty feet below. He could hear voices coming from down there, voices raised in anger. It sounded like Luce and Timilty all over again. *Isn't this where I came in?*

Spidey crawled closer to the open space at the warehouse's center. With any luck, he'd find some way to get Luce and Timilty out, and maybe find who was behind all this, too.

Fast Anthony had gotten out of the way just in time.

He'd been expecting Spider-Man. After all, that was why Stewart called him in and stationed him on the roof. "You're the one who gave us this," Stewart had said heartily. "We want you to run with it."

It had sounded like his big break at the time. It was only after Davis had climbed out onto the roof that he realized he might be the first one facing Spider-Man.

He started moving toward the air vent he had chosen as his hiding place as soon as he heard the limo pull up. As the loading-dock door noisily opened, he ran with all his strength toward the vent, the grinding of the motor below covering the sound of his sneakers pounding across the tar paper and gravel.

Spider-Man landed fifty feet in front of him, his back to the running Davis. Fast Anthony leapt forward, grabbing the lip of the metal vent and hauling himself inside. He waited close to two minutes, not even breathing, before he dared to look outside. The roof was empty. Spider-Man had already gone downstairs. He'd taken the first part of the bait.

Fast Anthony felt in his pocket to find the disposable camera was still there. *Good,* he thought. That was his insurance policy, after all, and it wouldn't do for him to lose it.

He hurried to follow the super hero.

Spidey carefully climbed out across one of the girders to get an unobstructed view of the scene below. The warehouse floor appeared empty save for Timilty, Luce, and that Andy character. The three of them were gathered around a speakerphone set up on a table, the sole piece of furniture on the entire cement floor.

Both Timilty and Luce were talking loudly. They were answered occasionally by a third voice coming from the speaker. The third, cultured voice sounded somehow familiar, but Spidey couldn't place it.

"This is ridiculous!" Timilty shouted. "You'll never get away with this!"

The disembodied voice replied: "Tyler Stewart gets away with whatever he wants."

Tyler Stewart? The man of the year? Mr. Money? Now, this was interesting. *Looks like Betty's instincts were on the money once again.*

The two people below kept on arguing, but it still all seemed pretty static down there now. They seemed to be waiting for something. When that something arrived, Spidey thought, then it would get really interesting.

While he waited, he set up his camera. Whatever was going on here, it qualified as news of some kind or other, particularly if Betty had found the facts to back up her hunch. He quickly positioned the Minolta to focus on Timilty, Luce, and whoever else might turn up. Stewart would be Spider-Man's first guess, but in a place like this, it could be anybody.

His spider-sense went crazy again. He looked up, to see a dozen goons running across the second floor, straight toward the girder where he was perched.

That's what they were waiting for, he thought as he prepared to spring into action. *Me.*

Nine

t was a trap.

Not that Spider-Man wasn't used to traps. He'd lost track of how often various super-villains had attempted to box him in or hang him up. On his own scale of traps, this one seemed pretty lame, maybe a three out of ten.

First off, he was hanging out over a twenty-foot drop on a six-inch-wide girder, which meant that, for the goons to get him, they would also have to walk along a six-inch-wide girder. And, unless a certain super hero was very much mistaken, no one up here with him had his sense of balance. Out over the middle of the floor, he presented a sitting target, but none of the goons now walking carefully toward him over half a dozen beams appeared to have a gun. Instead, Spidey saw plenty of lengths of pipe and chain. The plan, then, was to beat him senseless and take him alive. And what did this all have to do with Timilty and Luce, not to mention Tyler Stewart?

The girders crisscrossed half a dozen places around Spidey, as if they had been set up for a floor that was never laid. So the men now zeroing in on him could approach on parallel beams. But where Spider-Man now stood midgirder, only one goon could actually reach him from either side. All in all, it was a pretty good place to defend himself.

"Okay!" Spidey called out as the others cautiously approached. "First come, first served. Two fists, no waiting!"

If anything, his words seemed to slow his attackers down. The men in the lead looked to those who followed, then back at Spidey, and crept closer at little more than a snail's pace.

"Come on, guys," he said. "Let's get going here. What, you think I've got all night?"

With that, one bearded, heavyset guy with a length of chain strode forward. He swung the chain over his head as he moved toward Spider-Man.

"We're taking you down, wall-crawler!"

"Don't tell me," Spidey replied. "You thought up that sentence all by yourself." Just because they wanted him to be a sitting target didn't mean he had to oblige. Besides, this was all getting a little boring. "If you'll excuse me?"

He sent out a strand of webbing, which snagged one of another set of steel beams overhead. He tugged at the line to make sure it was firmly in place, then launched himself away from the man with the chain.

"Don't think this hasn't been fun," he yelled over his shoulder. "Because it—well, you know the rest."

Hey, if the thugs won't come to me, then I'll have to go to the thugs.

"Lights!" he called to those below. "Camera! Action!"

The men dove for the girders beneath them, hugging the metal for dear life as Spidey sailed overhead. Some of their pipes and other weapons clattered on the floor below.

Speaking of the floor below, Spidey thought, *I should take a peek at what happened to Mutt and Jeff.* If he was right, and all this was meant as a distraction, he wanted to get in on the real action downstairs with Luce and Timilty.

He landed lightly on the edge of the wooden flooring, a dozen men trying to turn around on the steel beams behind him.

Maybe I'll take the stairs.

"Got you!" a voice called.

He looked up and saw a large net dropping from above.

Somebody screamed.

Brian Timilty was surrounded by crazy people.

He and his manager had been dragged all over the city by a gun-toting, giggling loon. Then they had been brought to this nearly empty warehouse, to listen to more of Tyler Stewart's ramblings over a speakerphone. And now Spider-Man had shown up overhead, apparently not to rescue Timilty, but to fight with a dozen men directly above their heads.

"What the hell is going on here?" he demanded of the speakerphone.

Stewart's voice chuckled from the phone. "I suppose we could call it a floor show, except that it's happening on the ceiling. It's only a prelude to the real action. I call it the next step in your campaign, Brian."

"My campaign?" He glanced over at his campaign manager, standing between him and Stewart's man Andy. "I leave my campaign up to Luce!"

"Well," Stewart cheerfully agreed, "this will certainly be appropriate, then, because Michael Luce is going to help you like he never has before."

"Michael?" Timilty called. "What's going on?"

"I don't know, Brian," Luce replied. "I think that Stew has flipped his— No!"

Luce was staring at Andy, who no longer held a gun, nor his switchblade. Instead, Andy was holding what appeared to be a combat knife with a four-inch, serrated blade.

"Now, Andy," Stewart's voice instructed.

Andy closed the distance between himself and Luce with remarkable speed, diving beneath Luce's flailing hands.

Andy winked at Timilty as he plunged the knife deep into Luce's back. Luce screamed in pain as Andy backed away.

He left the knife behind.

Luce turned and looked at Timilty, his eyes wide with surprise.

"Brian?" he asked in a voice barely above a whisper.

Michael Luce fell forward into Timilty's arms.

No! Timilty thought. *It wasn't supposed to be like this. Luce and I are going to win this election together. Together!*

Luce groaned. Blood pumped from the wound in his back.

Timilty backed away. Luce slumped to the concrete floor. A pool of dark blood spread around him.

Timilty looked around the room. Andy had disappeared.

"Let that be a lesson to you, Brian," Stewart's voice announced from the speakerphone. "I don't let anybody call me Stew."

He broke the connection, a second's silence replaced by the constant whine of the dial tone.

"This way!"

Timilty turned around at the sound of the voice.

Devlin, the limousine driver, was standing in the doorway.

"You'll want to get out of here," Devlin called. "The police will be coming at any minute."

No. He couldn't be seen by the police. Not here, not like this. Timilty quickly ran away from the dying man.

A woman's voice followed him from the room: *"If you would like to make a call, please hang up and try again. If you need help, hang up and dial your—"*

The warehouse door slammed behind him. The limo was waiting.

What else could he do?

Spidey had jumped forward as soon as he had seen the net falling from above. He somersaulted across the floor until he reached the boxes. The heavy net had still managed to snag his foot, but only for a second. He shook himself free and looked around.

The goons had all made it off the crossbeams. But instead of attacking, they appeared to be running away, rushing down the same stairs Spidey was heading for. Apparently, a fair fight with Spider-Man had been too much for them.

Unless, of course, all of this was planned.

He heard, of all things, a dial tone coming from the speakerphone downstairs, replaced by that annoying recorded message you always got when your call went wrong.

What had happened to Timilty and Luce? He walked back to the drop-off at the center of the room.

He looked down to the floor below, and saw the body and the blood.

He heard a scream below. This was it. Show time.

Fast Anthony needed to do his thing.

Stewart's hired men went first, Spider-Man a moment later. Davis stepped out of his hiding place behind the boxes and quickly crawled out on the crossbeam to get the camera. He'd be fine as long as he could figure out how to override the remote control or automatic setting or whatever Spider-Man had it doing.

Spider-Man had pointed the camera right where Luce now lay in a pool of his own blood. Right where Spider-Man rushed to Luce's aid. *Perfect.*

Davis pressed the shutter release. It clicked. The camera worked like a charm. So did his disposable camera a moment later.

Davis smiled. This was going to be worth a lot to Mr. Stewart. He grabbed the camera and got off the crossbeam as quickly as he could. He wanted to get out while Spider-Man was still busy.

Perfect.

Spider-Man knew it was too late before he'd even reached the floor. The blood was spreading all over the concrete. Luce had rolled onto his side, the wound and the knife handle clearly visible.

He looked around the room as he landed, wary of another attack. But everything was still and empty. Everyone else was gone, Timilty included, as if they had never been here in the first place.

But they had left a man to die. He moved quickly to the fallen man's side, kneeling down to get a closer look at the damage.

Even if Luce had only one chance in a hundred, Spider-Man had to try to save him. Maybe he could find a way to slow the bleeding long enough to get him to a hospital. Better yet, he'd call an ambulance, so Luce didn't die on him on his way to being rescued.

Luce grabbed Spider-Man around the neck, trying to haul himself up. Spider-Man helped him rise to a sitting position. Luce groaned.

Spider-Man touched the hilt of the knife with a single gloved finger before pulling his hand away. Pulling a knife out of a wound like that would make it far worse. And he didn't want to mess up any fingerprints on the murder weapon.

"Why?" Luce moaned. He shuddered, and sagged down in Spider-Man's arms.

Spider-Man knew he was dead.

He was all alone with a corpse in a darkened warehouse. This, he knew, was the reason he had been brought here.

But why?

Ten

Peter Parker felt like he would never sleep again.

He had let Tyler Stewart lead him around. He had played right into his hands, but for what? So he could stand there and watch Michael Luce die?

He had been left with a dead man. Spider-Man had seen dozens of people die before, from total strangers to close friends and family, but it never got any easier, particularly when it was such a brutal and senseless murder.

Then, when Spider-Man had gone to retrieve his camera, it was gone. So any record he had had of Luce and Timilty and the actual killer together was gone, too.

On top of everything, the camera had been a special present to Peter from Mary Jane. Somehow, that bothered him as much as anything. He should never have taken it on

Spider-Man's rounds in the first place, or he should have gone without taking photos, or found some other way to get the money to repair his belt camera—he didn't know what he should have done. It did him no good to turn his anger in on himself like this. But what should he do?

There must have been some way he could have saved Luce's life. Someone had died, and here he was worried about his camera.

After Luce had died, Spider-Man had placed an anonymous call to the police and left. There was nothing else he could do.

He hadn't gotten home until two A.M. He spent what little was left of the night sitting in the living room, staring at the patterns in the hardwood floor.

A little after seven, Mary Jane came down from upstairs, kissed him on the forehead, and walked toward the front door, her slippered feet making a *shush shush shush* sound across the floor. She opened the front door to retrieve the morning paper.

"Oh, Peter!"

He looked up, startled for an instant from his funk. "What? What's wrong?"

She ran back into the living room, newspaper in hand. He didn't think he'd ever seen MJ look quite so upset.

"Peter?" she said, then again, "Peter?" as if she couldn't find any other words. She was staring at the front page of the *Bugle*.

She finally looked up at him. "Peter? What happened last night?"

He was on his feet, leaning over her shoulder.

There, on the front page of the *Bugle,* was a huge photo of Spider-Man with the dying Michael Luce in his arms. Above the photo, in large, black, sixty-point type, were three words: SPIDER-MAN: MURDERER?

Beneath the photo were a number of smaller blocks of type:

EXCLUSIVE PHOTOS SHOW SPIDER-MAN WITH DYING MICHAEL LUCE, MANAGER OF THE TIMILTY-FOR-MAYOR CAMPAIGN.

MORE INSIDE:

POLICE CALLED TO SCENE BY MYSTERIOUS PHONE CALL, PAGE 2.

MICHAEL LUCE: MYSTERY MAN WHO SPUN CAMPAIGN GOLD, PAGE 3.

THE SINISTER SPIDER-MAN: OTHER UNSOLVED MURDERS IN THE WEB-SLINGER'S PAST, PAGE 4.

SPECIAL J. JONAH JAMESON EDITORIAL: "VIGILANTE SUPER HEROES: THE THIN LINE BETWEEN JUSTICE AND MURDER."

"Peter," Mary Jane said, "what happened last night? It's like the newspaper already assumes you're the murderer."

It was worse than that. From the angle of the shot splashed across the front page, it looked like Spider-Man was grabbing the knife in Luce's back, perhaps even in the midst of plunging it in. With this photo showing up on every newsstand and doorstep of the city, everyone in greater New York would think he was the murderer.

"Peter," Mary Jane whispered. "Look at the credit on the photo. How could that be?"

Peter looked down at the small print below the lower right-hand corner of the picture. The photo was credited to Peter Parker!

This was beyond the Twilight Zone. Spider-Man had been condemned by his own alter ego.

Peter knew what had happened to his camera now. Somehow, after it had been stolen, the film inside had made it back to the *Bugle,* so they could run the photo on the next morning's front page.

That had been the real setup. First, to use Timilty and Luce as bait to lure Spider-Man in, then to keep the web-slinger busy long enough to fatally wound Luce, so that Spider-Man would go down to him and try to rescue a dying man. And then to take pictures of it all with Peter's own camera!

Peter felt like he had been kicked in the stomach. For this to work, someone would have to know an awful lot about Spider-Man.

"Peter," Mary Jane ordered. "Sit down. I want you to tell me everything."

Peter nodded and sat back down in his armchair. Mary Jane fetched a straight-backed chair from the dining room and sat directly in front of him.

She took his right hand in both of her own. "Now, tell me the whole story. We've got to figure out who did this to you, and how we can get Spider-Man out of trouble."

Peter briefly described the night before, just as he'd gone over it a hundred times in his head. Spotting Timilty and Luce, following the limo, finding them at the warehouse and learning Tyler Stewart was involved, setting up the camera just before the goons attacked, then trying to save the dying Luce.

"Why would someone do this?" MJ asked.

Peter had thought about that, too. "With his campaign manager killed by a super hero, Timilty is a shoo-in for mayor. And all the super heroes will probably be run out of town." That was something else that surprised him. He had thought Timilty no more than a loudmouthed politician. He had certainly never pegged Timilty as a murderer.

Mary Jane frowned. "Peter, how long have you been using that camera?"

"Only a couple of days, since the one on my belt broke." He thought of the feel of the Minolta in his hands and smiled wistfully. "It's a wonderful camera. I was trying to put some money together to get the belt camera fixed."

MJ tried to smile back. "I only get the best for my man. But who would know about a camera you had just barely begun to use?"

Peter hadn't even considered that. But there was a way he might be able to find out more. "Somehow, the film got to the *Bugle* under my name. Maybe Robbie can tell me something about who delivered it."

He reached for the phone and dialed the editor's direct line.

His editor picked it up on the third ring. "Robertson."

"Robbie, it's Peter Parker."

"Good to hear from you, son. We were a little worried after the way you left your camera here last night."

So the crooks had left both camera and film. How much of the truth could he tell Robbie? He'd have to act as natural as possible and find out as much as he could. "Well, that picture's part of a long story. So my camera's still there?"

"Betty's got it for you. I think she locked it in her desk."

There were so many people coming and going through the City Room, it was best to protect your valuables. The City Room was also so open that, as long as someone could get by the security guard downstairs, they probably could have dropped off the camera and film without anybody looking twice.

"When you had that messenger leave your camera here with the scribbled instructions for us to develop the film," Robbie continued, "I figured you must have been exhausted, maybe even hurt. After I saw the photos, I could see why you might have had enough."

That explained how they got past the security guard. If

the person dropping off the film claimed to be from one of the thousands of messenger services in the city, the guard would probably let them past without too much trouble.

Maybe, Peter thought, *it's time to tell Robbie a little more of the truth.* "Well, about the camera—"

A tinny but forceful voice interrupted in the background on Robbie's end. "Is that Parker on the phone?"

"Yes, Jonah, it—"

"Give me the phone, Robertson."

Peter heard a sigh, then Jonah's voice came in clearer. "Parker, I just wanted you to know that all is forgiven."

"Excuse me?" Peter said, confused.

"For that silly little outburst with Timilty. That may be the greatest photo you've ever taken in all the years you've been with the *Bugle!* We couldn't get it in the early editions, but we tore out the first five pages of the later edition to make room for this *wonderful* news. This is the sort of picture that wins awards, Parker. Great work!"

Awards? Yeah, what a combination; a Pulitzer prize and life in prison.

"Parker? You there?"

"Sure," Peter replied. "Just a little overwhelmed, I guess."

"Well, here's some more good news. Not only will you get your usual rate, but I'm even giving you a bonus. Finally, we've exposed that wall-crawling weasel for the murdering scum he really is!"

This was just too much. There was no way he could hold a coherent conversation. "Listen, Jonah, I'll talk to you later."

"Get down here when you can, my boy. I want you here when I announce the reward for information about Luce's murder, as well as for anyone who can provide information that leads to Spider-Man's arrest."

A reward? For Spider-Man?

"I'm glad everyone will get to see that that wall-crawling weasel's a cold-blooded murderer. Get down here as soon as you can, my boy."

Jonah hung up.

It was all too true. MJ had been right. Spider-Man had already been convicted in the press, thanks to a photo taken with his own camera.

The doorbell rang.

"I'll get it, Peter." Mary Jane stood up and walked from the room.

"Peter?" she called from the door. "It's the police. They say they want to talk to you."

He should have been expecting them. The photo credit on the first page of the *Bugle* said he was an eyewitness to the murder of Michael Luce.

Brian Timilty had always wanted power, but he never thought the price would be this high.

In the past, he had been willing to do certain favors for

Tyler Stewart. After all, the man had helped him rise through the ranks from community leader to city councillor to candidate for mayor—and maybe even the next mayor of New York. It had all seemed, if not innocent, at least ordinary—business as usual for a politician on his way up the ladder.

Until last night, when Timilty watched the murder of his own campaign manager.

It was a lesson. That was what Stewart had said when he'd called Timilty in the limo right after he and Devlin had left the warehouse. It was the most important lesson of all, to make it clear who had the real power in this political alliance. Michael Luce had failed to convince Timilty to listen to Stewart. Now Michael Luce was dead. Anyone who tried to stand between Stewart and his plans for running New York would suffer the same fate, whether it was Timilty, his ex-wife, his daughter, his girlfriend, anyone that meant anything to Timilty.

As Stewart continued to talk in the same cheerful tone, one thing became abundantly clear to Timilty: Stewart was indeed capable of anything.

"You know," Stewart had said at the end of the conversation, "you may think you're indispensable here, but you're the most disposable part of my plan. Sure, like I told you the other day, it might slow down my plans a little if you don't become mayor. But there're always other up-and-comers looking to improve their power base, and their lifestyle. You do like your new brownstone, don't you, Brian? You wouldn't want to lose it to the next candidate ready to sell their services to the highest bidder?"

Timilty felt like he'd sold far more than his services.

But what could he do? If he went to the police, news of his involvement with Stewart would cost him the election. And after what had happened to Luce, he was sure Stewart would make good on his threats and kill everyone Timilty held dear.

There was no way out.

Stewart had him in a box. Only a day ago, he was looking forward to the election, to at least four glorious years in Gracie Mansion. Now, thanks to a single, horrible moment, his dream had become a nightmare. Every day he was mayor of New York, he would see the dying Luce.

What could Timilty do? His campaign manager had orchestrated Timilty's every move, chosen every sound bite. Without Luce's guidance, Timilty was lost.

"You need me far more than I need you," Stewart had said. With Luce gone, that was doubly true. He would hate Stewart, he would fear Stewart, but Stewart would tell him what to do, and he'd do it.

At least he didn't have to smile for the cameras for the next few hours. Timilty had called his campaign headquarters and told them to cancel everything until noon, to give him time to recover "from his shocking loss," as he'd put it. He had instructed Luce's assistant, Sasha, to write a short speech expressing his grief and anger over these terrible events. Somehow, after that, he'd learn to carry on.

He would soon be mayor of New York City. He would learn to smile again.

Eleven

Peter wondered how many times in a five-hour period you could repeat the same story, because that's how many times he had answered the questions of these two detectives.

Peter Parker was nowhere near the warehouse. His camera had been stolen. He hadn't reported it because it happened only yesterday. No, he didn't drop the camera off at the *Bugle,* nor did he hire the messenger that did bring it. Yes, he had an association with Spider-Man. He made a major part of his living taking pictures of the super hero. But he and Spider-Man didn't hang out and talk. Spider-Man wouldn't tell anybody, Peter included, about his secret identity.

Yes, Peter did get into an argument with Timilty and Luce at the *Bugle* the other day. Yes, it was a heated argument, but nobody threw any punches. Besides, just because you have words with someone doesn't mean you want somebody dead. Besides, his words were with Timilty, not Luce. He barely knew Luce was in the room.

He had spent the evening at home with his wife. No, he had no idea where Spider-Man might be hiding.

Peter was angry, hungry, and tired. Besides that little white lie about being home with his wife, he tried to tell as much of the truth as he could without exposing his secret identity.

The two cops, Briscoe and Logan, just wouldn't let up. Each of them had a style that complemented the other's. Briscoe was the shouter, pushing his large, beer-bellied frame around the room, trying to bully something out of Peter, while Logan, his thinner, smaller counterpart, spoke softly, trying to trick him into saying a bit more than he had planned.

A couple of times they'd gotten Peter a drink of water, but mostly it was just the three of them in a small, drab room somewhere in the bowels of One Police Plaza in lower Manhattan, a light on Peter's face, as he heard the same questions over and over again. Peter had spent time in interrogation rooms before, most recently as Spider-Man when cooperating with the NYPD. He wondered if that would ever happen again. *After last night, probably not.*

"This guy is wasting our time!" Briscoe shouted for maybe the seventh time. "Why don't we throw him in a cell overnight and see if he opens up?"

"Oh, I think we have other ways to handle this," Logan replied smoothly. He looked to Peter. "Shall we go over this again?"

"Look, I've been as cooperative as I can be for five hours," Peter snapped. "I can't do any more. I need to know if you're going to press charges."

"Charges for what?" Logan asked innocently.

"For whatever you brought me down here for. Are you going to charge me with something, or can I walk away?"

Logan shook his head. "Parker, all we're trying to get at here is the truth. You may even know Spider-Man a bit better than you're willing to let on." He looked to his partner. "You can go, but we're going to keep an eye on you."

Peter stood up. "I suppose I shouldn't think about leaving town anytime soon, huh?"

It was Briscoe who laughed. "And they say college students aren't getting any brighter these days."

Mary Jane was waiting for him by the admittance desk.

Peter was simultaneously overjoyed to see her and upset that she had to spend her entire day waiting for him.

"You've been sitting here all day?" he asked after she'd given him a big hug.

"Well, I did take a couple of walks to the bathroom and the precinct snack machines, but besides that, I've been waiting for you." She patted a textbook she carried under her arm. "I did catch up on my psych reading. So how are you?" She was trying to smile, but Peter could see the worry in her eyes.

"Well, they let me go, at least for now. I'm exhausted. Let's get out of here."

It was the middle of the afternoon by the time they walked out of the station. He felt like it should be the middle of the night. He'd rather go one-on-one with Dr. Octopus than have to go through another day like this.

Mary Jane asked Peter if he'd like something to eat. Suddenly, he was very hungry. They found a coffee shop and went inside. They easily got a table; the last of the lunch-hour crowd was just leaving.

As soon as they sat down, Mary Jane pulled a newspaper out of her purse. "I thought you'd want to know about this. I picked it up the one time I left the station for some air. The *Bugle* printed an extra edition."

She handed him the new paper with a brand-new front page. The headline read, BUGLE OFFERS REWARD: $5000 FOR SPIDER-MAN.

The art department had set up the page a lot like those "Wanted: Dead or Alive" posters one always sees on those Westerns on American Movie Classics.

Suddenly, Peter's appetite was gone. They were wasting no time in making Spidey a wanted man.

The waitress arrived. Mary Jane ordered a salad. Peter said he wanted only a cup of coffee, but at his wife's urging, broke down and ordered a chicken salad sandwich, too. The waitress brought the coffee for Peter and a glass of water for MJ, then disappeared through a swinging door.

MJ waved at the paper. "I didn't want to show you this while you were still at the police station."

"A good thing, too." Peter tried to smile. "I would have shouted so loud, they would have locked me up for disturbing the peace."

"But there's got to be something we can do," Mary Jane insisted. "We never got to finish our talk at home."

She was right. The police had shown up before they really had a chance to hash things out. Peter shook his head, really smiling this time. He didn't know what he would do without Mary Jane to calm him down.

"So what do you know about all this, Peter?" MJ prompted. "Did the police tell you anything new?"

Peter shook his head. "I'm the only one who knows about Timilty's connection with Stewart. Stewart's the one behind all of this. He was the one ordering the guy with the gun around. He was the one that ordered Luce killed."

Mary Jane twirled a strand of red hair around her index finger, momentarily lost in thought. She looked back at Peter. "But if you go to the police with that information—"

"They'll know I was there. And that opens a whole other can of worms. Given that kind of information, they might be able to figure out I'm somewhat . . . closer to Spider-Man than I generally let on. At the very least, they'd probably charge me with hindering a criminal investigation. I could end up spending a month or two in jail."

"You have some friends on the force—maybe one of

them could help out?" MJ sounded unconvinced of her statement even as she said it.

It was true, Spider-Man had made a few allies on the NYPD. A couple of years back, Spidey had caught the killer of Jean DeWolff, a beloved captain; more recently, he'd been instrumental in saving another captain, Frank Esteban, from a group of terrorists. It was tempting to call Esteban or one of the other cops he had become friendly with, but probably a bad idea. "I doubt any of them would be willing to help out. The best I can hope for is that, if one of them happens to see me, they probably won't shoot me down."

Mary Jane sighed and looked down at the newspaper between them. "A reward? What was Jameson thinking? Every gun nut in New York is going to be out—"

"Hunting for spiders," Peter agreed. "I think sometimes Jonah cares only about selling papers."

"So that's what this reward is? A publicity stunt?"

"Oh, Jonah believes in what he's doing. But he wouldn't even try it if he didn't think he'd replace the reward with newspaper revenues. That's the way his brain works."

They stopped talking for a moment as the waitress returned to the table with their order. She glanced at the two of them, and at the plate in either hand. "So let's see. The salad for you, hon"—she placed a large bowl in front of Mary Jane—"and a chicken salad sandwich for the man with no appetite."

She frowned down at the headline of the newspaper on the table. "Isn't it terrible what that Spider-Man did? It's about time we got his sort off the streets." She looked at Peter and Mary Jane and smiled. "Well, you kids let me know if I can get you anything else."

She turned away and marched back through the swinging door.

Peter sighed. "So even the waitresses are out to get Spider-Man."

Mary Jane picked up her fork and studied her salad. "I've got an idea. Maybe Spider-Man has to lie low, but that doesn't mean that we have to. Maybe it's time for the two of us to play hero and rescue Spider-Man for a change."

"But I really think I've got a lead here," Betty Brant insisted. Across from her in the conference room, Ben Urich and Robbie Robertson didn't look as impressed as she wanted them to.

"It sure is interesting," Ben agreed. "But right now, it's still circumstantial. It's just about impossible to get a member of Stewart's camp to talk about anything. Trust me on this. I've tried."

"They're that loyal?" Betty asked. If the *Bugle*'s number-one crime reporter couldn't get something out of these people, what hope did she have of getting the story?

"No." Ben ran a hand through his salt-and-pepper hair. Betty glanced at the sleeve of his rumpled sport coat. Either he wore the same coat to the office every day, or he had a closet full of them, and he slept in them to give them the proper wrinkled look. "It's not loyalty that keeps them quiet, it's fear. Somebody in Stewart's organization is not entirely kosher. It may even be Stewart himself. And, according to your information, Timilty and Stewart may have a very close connection. Is Stewart dirty? Does he have Timilty in his pocket? It would be a great story if you could get the pieces to fit."

Robbie shook his head as he puffed on his pipe. "It's just got to be rock solid. Especially now. In the public's mind, our front-page story proves Timilty was right about super heroes. Spider-Man looks like a loose cannon. If he wasn't directly responsible for Luce's murder, he was certainly somehow involved. And Luce becomes a martyr to Timilty's cause."

Betty almost laughed. "Michael Luce a martyr? I never thought I'd see the day."

"Hey," Ben said, "we live in a society where Richard Nixon became an honored elder statesman. We all know that Luce was at the very least a media manipulator, and probably was responsible for a lot of dirty tricks against the opponents of all of his candidates. I've found twenty-one separate items, including a couple with people opposed to Timilty. Unfortunately, I've been having the same problem proving that Luce is responsible that Betty's been having proving that Stewart's dirty."

Robbie puffed on his pipe. "Right now, it just seems to be a coincidence. We certainly can't go around kicking a fresh corpse without something more solid."

Ben nodded. "I'll interview some of the opponents, at least the ones that are still alive."

"Some of them died?" Betty asked incredulously.

"Two. One was an accident, the other one committed suicide after things about him were revealed by anonymous sources."

Robbie even smiled at that. "We may be able to build a real case here. But the story right now is Luce's death, not his life—and Spider-Man's involvement in that death. That's what's going to sell tomorrow's edition of the *Bugle,* and that's what Jonah wants us to follow up on. Betty, Ben, check your facts, get me some additional proof, and maybe we can blow open a whole new story about Stewart and Timilty and Luce in a few days." He took another puff, then added, "Photos would be good, too. Maybe you could get Peter to give you a hand."

"If the cops ever let him go," Ben allowed.

"The *Bugle* might have to take on that crusade, too. We can't have New York's finest interfering with the freedom of the press. Let me know if they charge him with anything."

Betty was worried about her old friend, too. Peter had been wonderfully helpful when Betty worked to clear the name of her deceased husband Ned Leeds, who had been accused of being the super-villain known as the Hobgoblin. Spider-Man had helped out then, too. Maybe she was letting her personal feelings get in the way of her reporting, but she couldn't imagine either of them involved in the murder of Michael Luce.

But if Spider-Man hadn't killed Luce, then who had?

Betty knew that, somehow, Tyler Stewart was the key to all of this. According to Robbie, they might be able to blow the whistle on Luce and Stewart within the week.

She hoped, for Peter's sake, that a week from now wouldn't be too late.

The Rhino was sick and tired of waiting. First, these two guys had dressed up as cops and masterminded his escape, telling him he was going to meet with this Tyler Stewart jerk. But then this Stewart had never shown.

Instead, Rhino and the two guys who weren't cops holed up in an old motel out near Kennedy Airport. They had banged out the walls between a couple of the rooms to make it one large suite, even given Rhino a king-size bed so he had someplace decent to sleep.

The place was still a dump.

These would probably be the last rooms rented in all of greater New York. There didn't seem to be anybody staying here now besides Rhino and his two keepers. He bet Stewart owned the whole motel.

He'd been here for the better part of three days. And he still hadn't had the heart-to-heart with Stewart that the two noncops had promised. Oh, they had trucked him out the other night to that park on the other side of Queens, saying they needed him for a little "intimidation."

All he did was stand back in the shadows. He hadn't even met Stewart personally. And he was supposed to intimidate Electro? The electric guy could probably fry him in place before Rhino could even reach him to toss him across the room.

And after that? The guys had brought him back here.

His main keepers were a pair of guys named Spike and Jeremiah. Not Jerry—Jeremiah liked the whole name. Mostly he sat in front of the TV, even though they only ran the same four movies over and over again. Spike, on the other hand, liked to play gin rummy. Most of the time, Rhino let Spike win. It wasn't like they were playing for money.

Rhino supposed this was better than prison, but not much. He couldn't go anywhere for fear of being recognized, and all Spike and Jeremiah brought in to eat was fast food from around the neighborhood. In prison, at least you got vegetables. This whole scene was getting old very fast.

And still there was no sign of Stewart.

"Is that someone outside?" Spike asked as he dealt another hand. How Spike could hear cars over the planes constantly taking off and landing was beyond the Rhino.

Jeremiah moved the curtain aside to look out the window.

"Hey, Devlin's here. And it looks like he's brought you a present."

He got up from his chair across from the TV and walked briskly to the front door.

"Tommy!" he called. "What's shakin'?"

"Not much," the tall newcomer admitted as he struggled to get into the door with a large suitcase. "How are the movies?"

Jeremiah shrugged. "I've seen better. What's in the case?"

Devlin grinned. "It's a little present for our esteemed guest." He placed the suitcase in front of the Rhino. "Here."

The Rhino unzipped the large piece of luggage to reveal a brand-new Rhino suit inside.

"The boss is particularly pleased with this one," Devlin added. "He researched your old suits from some police files we managed to borrow, then got a couple of his boys in one of his research-and-development units to improve it a little. This skin should be every bit as tough as—well, when you used to have a Rhino skin of your own."

Rhino ran his hand over the material, rock hard and flexible at the same time.

"No more gin rummy for you," Devlin said with a grin. "The boss says it's time to put you to work."

Rhino looked from the suit to Devlin and back again. What did they expect him to do, just follow orders?

Maybe this wasn't any better than prison after all.

Twelve

eter walked out of the kitchen, a bowl of munchies in either hand, to see his wife and Ben Urich staring at each other from across the room.

Ben took the cigarette out of his mouth. "You *do* mind if I smoke, don't you?"

Behind Peter, Betty Brant started to laugh. Ben Urich was the living embodiment of the hard-bitten crime-beat reporter, down to the two-pack-a-day cigarette habit; five minutes after he'd stubbed one smoke out, another cigarette had found its way to the corner of his mouth. It was only when Ben looked over the flame of his Zippo lighter that he realized there might be a problem.

"Yes, I do mind," Mary Jane said with a self-deprecating grin. "It's funny. Ever since I stopped smoking, I can't stand the smell."

Ben shrugged. "It happens a lot. Sometimes I wish it happened to me." He stuck the cigarette back in the pack. "I'll have one of these later—outside."

"So let's get to work," Betty announced as Peter put the two bowls down on the coffee table and took a seat on the couch next to Mary Jane. Both Betty and Ben sat in a pair of overstuffed chairs, solid furniture left over from the days when aunt May and uncle Ben owned the house.

"We know why we're here," Betty continued, "to get at what really happened to Michael Luce—"

"Not to mention keeping Peter out of jail," Ben added.

"Sounds good to me," Betty added with a nod. "How do we break the real story?"

Mary Jane glanced over at the television. They had WNN on to see if anything developed.

"Peter," MJ said, "this is what we were waiting for." She grabbed the remote from the table and turned up the sound.

"We now take you to the special press conference at City Hall, held at the request of Manhattan District Attorney Blake Tower. And now to our reporter on the scene, Jen Trynin. Jen?"

The scene switched to an attractive young woman with a slightly fussy hairstyle and a little too much makeup. She held a microphone and stood in what looked like a hallway at City Hall.

"Thanks, Wannetta," the reporter said in the most serious of tones. "Speculation runs rampant here at City Hall as the mayor's office tries to determine whether Spider-Man is indeed implicated in the death of political consultant Michael Luce. The situation is complicated by the fact that Luce was working for the mayor's strongest challenger in the upcoming election, Brian Timilty, so both the incumbent and the DA's office will have to act swiftly and decisively in this matter to avoid charges of political favoritism. No matter what happens here today, Timilty appears to be the clear political winner, as his claims of super heroes being nothing more than lawless vigilantes seem proven by these recent events. With the election less than two weeks away . . ." The reporter paused and put a hand up to her ear. "I have just received word that the press conference is about to start."

The scene shifted to the City Hall briefing room, where the cultured, blond-haired Blake Tower stood behind a podium bearing the city seal.

"Ladies and gentlemen of the press," Tower began, "and the citizens of New York City." He looked directly into the camera. "In the past twenty-four hours, thanks to the reportage of the *Daily Bugle,* we have all been witness to the death of Michael Luce by a knife wound to the back. According to a preliminary coroner's report, this wound punctured Luce's lung and produced other internal damage, causing the victim to bleed to death in a matter of minutes." He took a deep breath. "While not well known to the public, Mr. Luce was recognized by most of those in public office in our city, and had been instrumental in aiding many of our elected officials in obtaining their chosen office. Many of those in this office, City Hall, and the state legislature feel the loss of Mr. Luce deeply. This murder cuts at the very political process that keeps us strong, and will be dealt with swiftly and decisively."

"Wait a minute," Ben interjected. "Is he saying political consultants are good for democracy?"

Tower droned on: "I am here to tell you what the DA's office intends to do about this case. First, Spider-Man will be brought in for questioning. If the evidence warrants, he will be arrested and tried. Super heroes aren't a law unto themselves. We need to reassert that we are a city and a nation of law, and anyone who flouts those laws upon which this country was built will be dealt with in the harshest manner possible. Thank you."

He looked out over the audience. "I will now take some of your questions."

"Mr. Tower," Ben muttered softly, "do you know the meaning of the words *witch hunt?*"

Two dozen reporters shouted, all trying to be heard.

He picked a woman in the front row.

"Margie?" he called.

"How do you plan to detain Spider-Man?" Margie asked. Peter recognized her as a reporter for the *Daily Globe.*

"Well, as I mentioned in my statement, we first have to determine if Spider-Man was indeed involved in the murder. After all, *anyone* could wear a Spider-Man costume if they wished to frame the super hero. We have experts examining both the photographic evidence and the scene of the crime for more conclusive proof of guilt."

Wait a minute, Peter thought. *They're examining the photographic evidence? What photographic evidence?* "Did Jonah give the police my negatives?" Peter asked aloud.

"Are you kidding?" Betty replied. "He must have those negatives locked in his safe. Jonah wouldn't give away anything he could use unless he was subpoenaed, and sometimes not even then."

"They're probably studying the photos the *Bugle* sent out over the wire," Ben added. "But what do you mean, *your* negatives? I thought you said the camera was stolen and somebody else got those shots."

He had given Betty and Ben the same story he had given to the police. After all, the camera *had* been stolen, just a little bit later than he let on.

"It's still my camera and my negatives, no matter who took the pictures," Peter said, doing his best to keep his voice calm.

"Here's the bottom line on Spider-Man," Tower was saying. "If he is listening, I would like to personally ask him to turn himself in to the nearest precinct now for questioning, so that we can determine his involvement in this matter, if any, once and for all. Next question?"

A man Peter didn't recognize at all stood next, probably somebody from one of the networks or national news services. After all, the possibility that Spider-Man was a murderer was big-time news.

The man quickly asked his question: "Spider-Man has been charged with murder before, for the death of retired police captain George Stacy. In light of recent events, do you regret dropping the earlier charges?"

"Certainly not," Tower replied. "That was an entirely different case. The evidence gathered by my office in that investigation indisputably showed that Dr. Otto Octavius, the man known to the public as Dr. Octopus, was clearly responsible for Captain Stacy's death. I stand by that decision."

Mary Jane chewed on her lower lip as she watched the coverage. She turned back to Peter. "Tower looks like he's doing his best to be fair."

"He has that reputation," Ben agreed. "But it won't do him much good in the next election if he's wrong about Spider-Man."

Or, Peter thought, *if the rest of the public is convinced he was wrong about Spider-Man.* He couldn't get Urich's earlier comment about "witch hunt" out of his head, either.

Tower's face was abruptly replaced by a blue card with yellow lettering: BULLETIN.

"We're interrupting our coverage of the press conference to bring you a late-breaking story on the streets of Manhattan."

The scene cut back to the anchorwoman in the WNN studio.

"WNN brings you this report, live, from the corner of Sixth Avenue and Forty-seventh Street. We now take you to the scene with reporter Steve Roman."

A young, well-tanned blond man appeared on the screen, standing with a microphone on a Manhattan street corner. "Thank you, Wannetta. Police have cordoned off this section of Manhattan, popularly known as the Diamond District, as the costumed super-villain known as the Rhino has gone on a rampage, smashing his way from store to store, stealing every diamond in sight."

The camera panned right to show a street littered with glass and twisted metal. Peter could hear the sounds of police sirens and people shouting. The camera's picture bounced up and down as its operator moved farther around the corner.

"We're going to try to get a closer look at the devastation here," the reporter continued, "obviously not just huge losses in stolen diamonds, but in property damage as well. Wait a minute! There's something happening farther down the street! I think it's the Rhino!"

The picture swung farther down the street, to a pair of uniformed police officers, their weapons drawn, shouting at someone just offscreen.

Both of them took a few stumbling steps backward as the Rhino entered the picture. He dwarfed both of the cops with his huge seven-foot-plus frame in the wrinkled gray Rhino costume, complete with two nasty horns atop his head. The Rhino lumbered on, pushing the cops aside as he would swat away a pair of flies, barely worth his notice. The bullets the cops fired seemed to have no effect on his Rhino suit.

The Rhino bellowed and turned, lowering his horns to crash into the next shop on the block.

"And people ask me why I live in New York City." Ben shook his head. "Never a dull moment, huh?"

The reporter's breathless voice resumed. "As is readily apparent, the police appear powerless to stop this raging super-villain. Without some other outside intervention, it appears the Rhino will be able to do whatever he wants to New York's Diamond District."

Peter realized he was standing. The Rhino was destroying Manhattan. And where was Spider-Man? Miles away in Forest Hills, trying to save his own skin.

He felt a hand on his arm. He looked up to see Mary Jane frowning at him in concern.

"Peter? Could you help me in the kitchen for a second?"

He knew exactly what she was going to say. His agitation was much too obvious. Spider-Man could get upset, but Peter Parker had to take this in stride. Well, maybe it was time for Peter to make his excuses and for Spidey to go into action.

Mary Jane took him by the arm and marched him into the other room.

"Look, Peter," she began as soon as the door to the living room was closed. "I know what's going through that heroic head of yours. But you can't go after the Rhino, not now. Those police are all armed, and considering what has been in the papers lately, they are almost more likely to take a shot at you than they are at the Rhino."

Peter felt trapped, helpless. He wanted to shout, but managed to keep his voice low. "But I can't sit by and watch Rhino tear up every street in New York! The people—"

MJ folded her arms in front of her. "By the time you traveled from Forest Hills to Manhattan, who's to say the Rhino would even be there anymore? Manhattan is crawling with super heroes. And here it is on the news for everyone to see. Let the Avengers or the Fantastic Four or Heroes for Hire or the New Warriors or even the Black Cat take care of this one."

Peter took a deep breath. It went against every single thing he'd stood for since he'd been Spider-Man. But this time Mary Jane was right. It made no sense to expose Spider-Man to a crime he would be too late to stop anyway.

"So let's go back and talk with our guests," MJ concluded. "After all, we're doing this for Spider-Man, and you, too."

Peter nodded. Mary Jane was talking sense. As much

trouble as he would have sitting still, it was dangerous out there for Spider-Man right now.

MJ opened the door that led to the living room. "Does anyone want some more coffee?" She grabbed the pot and waved for Peter to follow her.

"They've gone back to the press conference," Betty said as they walked back into the room. "The reporters are asking about Luce now. Tower doesn't seem to know any more than anybody else about our favorite political consultant." She shook her head. "Before Michael Luce became a political handler about five years ago, he seems to have had no past at all."

Ben grinned at that. "Which means he's probably got a very interesting past, and we're just the folks to find it." He shook his head too. "Never has a weasel been so eloquently mourned. And Luce was a weasel."

The press conference disappeared from the TV screen, replaced once again by the bulletin sign.

"WNN has learned there have been new developments in the Diamond District," the anchorwoman began. "Let's go back to Steve Roman on the scene."

The scene cut to the tanned blond reporter again, standing in the middle of the rubble-strewn street. "Thank you, Wannetta. The destruction of the Diamond District has taken on a dramatic turn as the NYPD has called in their special Code Blue squad, an elite fighting force specially trained to deal with individuals with super powers. We understand that the Code Blue team has managed to halt the

Rhino's rampage. Ah! Here's team leader Lieutenant David Marshall. Lieutenant Marshall! Can you tell us anything about the progress of your operation?"

The camera shifted left to include a thin, intense black man in blue riot gear who glared at the camera.

"We expect to have the Rhino in custody shortly," Marshall replied. "While he has temporarily gotten past our men, our elite tracking—"

"They've lost him?" Ben shouted incredulously. "How can you lose someone as large as the Rhino?"

Peter winced. No matter what the difficulty, or the danger, he couldn't get over the feeling that Spider-Man should have been there.

"Maybe we should turn that off," Betty suggested. "As amusing as the NYPD's Three Stooges impressions can be, we've got a job to do." She looked at the food spread out on the table in front of her. "I say it's time to eat a few corn curls and try to figure out how we're going to break the story of the century."

This was most unsatisfactory.

Tyler Stewart pressed a button on his desk control unit, turning off the TV monitor he'd installed over the bar.

The Rhino, he supposed, had done his part, smashing and crashing through downtown Manhattan until he had escaped with a few million dollars' worth of diamonds. Diamonds, frankly, Stewart had never expected to obtain.

This whole drama was supposed to flush Spider-Man

out into the open, not give the NYPD a chance to wave around a bunch of big guns that would drive the Rhino away. Stewart had expected the web-slinger to confront that lumbering brute, the two of them duking it out just long enough for the police to arrest both of them. Then, while Spider-Man was in custody, Stewart would use his connections inside the Ryker's Island facility to deal with the super hero once and for all.

But the Rhino was stronger and faster than Stewart had thought, and Spider-Man hadn't even bothered to show up. Maybe the wall-crawler *was* the self-serving vigilante the papers made him out to be.

Or maybe this whole thing was too obvious a trap. After all, Spider-Man had been wanted by the police before, and that had never stopped him from going about his usual business. So he would have stayed away from this only if he knew it was a setup.

Stewart sighed. The Rhino would hand over the diamonds to his people shortly. It was always nice to have a little extra cash. But Stewart wanted Spider-Man instead.

Tyler Stewart had always been very careful about choosing his employees. These recent events had caused him to lower his standards slightly. He hoped he wouldn't regret those decisions.

First, there was Fast Anthony Davis. So far, he'd done everything Stewart had asked him to do. But Stewart also remembered why, two years before, he had decided to drop

Fast Anthony from his organization. Davis was too clever, and ambitious in all the wrong ways. The young man was a quick learner, maybe too quick. He always had a "better" way of doing things. If Stewart had given him enough power, Davis would have eventually challenged Mr. Money for his whole organization.

Of course, that was a couple years back, when Stewart's mob hadn't quite gained its current respectable veneer. The organization was much larger now, too. Perhaps there was a place for Davis in the current setup for a while, doing dangerous jobs like stealing a camera from Spider-Man. And, if Davis started getting pushy again, well, Andy doubly enjoyed killing people he knew.

Stewart stared at the now-blank television monitor. For all his worry about ambitious street punks, super-villains were even worse. Oh, someone like the Rhino was not very bright, and could be easily manipulated. Electro, on the other hand, was too used to being his own boss, and drunk on his control of electricity.

Right now, Stewart and Electro had reasons to help each other. But as soon as the electric man got what he wanted, Stewart was sure that Electro would not hesitate to betray him or any of his men. Fine. Electro still owed Stewart a favor. And the minute that Stewart had gotten what he could out of the high-powered crook, he'd get a sniper to put a bullet in his brain.

He just had to remember, every problem had a solution.

And every solution brought Stewart that much closer to where he wanted to be.

Soon, he'd be too big for anybody—Electro, Spider-Man, the NYPD, or even the mayor of New York—to bring him down.

Thirteen

The time was finally here.

Max Dillon looked at the photostats. Tyler Stewart was a thorough man, and he delivered. Dillon had everything he needed before him now—maps, descriptions, and diagrams, all the information the Department of Water and Power had on the pumps that sent fresh water to the five boroughs from the upstate reservoirs.

It was the simplest of ideas, really. But then, weren't the simple ideas always the best? He smiled at the diagrams of the pumps, and the maps showing their exact locations, with the best access routes to the pumps drawn in yellow marker. It was sort of like an AAA guide to New York City's sewers.

With this information, it would be child's play to shut

down the pumps. And even a child knew what would happen next.

After all, you couldn't run a city without water.

He leaned back, savoring his surroundings. This room had never looked so warm and cozy, the interesting cracks that ran through the plaster, the abstract beauty of the sun-faded prints over the bed, the sport of frying what few foolhardy cockroaches remained. Such a simple place to hatch such a lucrative plan.

And for all this, Electro wanted only a billion dollars. A small price to pay to keep New York from going dry.

And Stewart was in this with him all the way. Originally, Electro had thought he'd get Fast Anthony to gather a few more trustworthy individuals for the night of the job, people Davis knew from the street. Max Dillon wanted to depend on as few other people as possible. But Stewart had a whole organization to call on, an organization that they could trust to do the job.

Stewart got something out of it too, of course. After all, any delay on the mayor's part brought public opinion down against the current mayor and doubly guaranteed Timilty's election, putting a brand-new mayor in Stewart's pocket. And, when the delivery had come from Stewart, there had been a note attached, telling Electro that Stewart expected a "good-faith finder's fee" for the information, ten percent of whatever Electro received.

Electro was surprised to see that Stewart wasn't exactly clear on who was blackmailing whom. When this was all over, he planned to meet with Stewart personally. He imagined the self-styled boss of New York would find the meeting positively shocking.

But for now, the plan was perfect. Even Spider-Man was out of the way, on the run from the police. Electro looked down at the wanted poster on the front of the *Bugle*. He wondered how Spider-Man felt having the tables turned on him, to go from crusading hero to wanted felon. All that really mattered was that Spider-Man was effectively out of the way. Unless the wanted man was foolish enough to show up and try to foil Electro's plans. Maybe, Dillon thought, he could even bring down Spider-Man. Then Electro, of all people, could be a hero for a day.

Max Dillon smiled. Now the excitement would begin. People would die. New York City would be brought to its knees. But most of all, it was time for Electro to become very, very rich.

JOSIE'S BAR.

Besides that one small, pink neon sign in one small, grubby window, Peter would have expected this building to be empty and abandoned. Everything else on the outside was painted black and boarded over.

"Wow," Peter said to Ben Urich as the other man opened the black wooden door. "Now, this place looks inviting. No wonder I don't drink."

Ben chuckled. "They're not big on tourists in a place like Josie's. It's not as bad as it looks. They tend not to kill people in the bar proper. That would bring the police."

Ben was obviously having a good time with this. They were on his turf now. Peter wasn't sure if he should have new respect for the crime-beat reporter or worry about his sanity.

He followed Ben from the nighttime street into an interior that looked even darker. The first door didn't lead into the bar proper. They walked down a short, dark hallway, lit by a tiny grimy yellow lightbulb. At least outside there had been a streetlight.

This was the third bar Ben and he had walked into, each one a little sleazier than the one before. The last two places had been dives, holes in the wall where people peered suspiciously at you through far too much cigarette smoke.

Ben had been saving Josie's for last. He would only say that things could "get a little serious" in a place like that.

"Don't worry," he added. "I've taken photographers to some of my haunts before, and I haven't gotten one killed yet."

Peter decided this was one of those days he was very happy to have hidden super powers.

Ben pushed his way through a second door. Peter could hear the noise of the actual bar beyond. It was a little brighter in here. The room was bigger than the past couple of joints, but the cigarette smoke was every bit as thick. A number of people were talking and laughing. The two pool tables in the back were occupied. Music was playing in the background, some disco tune from the seventies.

Ben stepped into the bar. A couple of people looked over and nodded. Peter walked into the room, and all the conversation stopped. The disco song thumped to a conclusion thirty seconds later.

Peter didn't think he'd ever heard such total silence.

This was like when the sheriff walked into the saloon in one of those old Westerns. It felt like everybody was waiting to see who would be the first one to pull a gun.

Ben looked over at the bar.

"Phil," he called. "This is Peter. He's with me."

The man behind the bar nodded and went back to wiping out the insides of his glassware with a rag. Half a dozen conversations sprung up around them. Another disco song started thumping somewhere behind them.

"Well, we passed that test." Ben waved for Peter to follow him to an empty table in the corner.

"We don't want to look any more conspicuous than we have to," Ben said as they reached their table. "What would you like to drink?"

He had to drink? He guessed that meant they were staying here awhile. This place would give even Spider-Man the creeps. People were talking, but that didn't mean that half the occupants of this bar still weren't watching him, and about half of those seemed to keep one of their hands very close to a pocket or a bulge beneath their sport coats.

One false move, and Peter was sure he'd see twenty or thirty guns and knives. He had a feeling that his spider-sense was going to go wild at any second.

"Peter?" Ben prompted as Peter sat down at the tiny table. He looked up at his friend.

"Just a Coke, I guess."

"Nothing harder, huh? Boy, you'd make a lousy crime reporter. You're almost as pure as those super heroes you're always taking pictures of." Ben chuckled as he left Peter alone at the table and walked over to the bar to fetch a couple drinks.

Peter did his best to look around the room without appearing to look around. A lot of the men in here looked like Spider-Man might have left them in an alley somewhere, wrapped in webbing as a present for the police. But some of the men were quite well dressed, and others wouldn't have been out of place on a college campus. There were some fabulous-looking women, too. Most of the latter probably made their living out on the streets. It was a whole different world in here. The only contact Spider-Man would have had with most of the gentlemen in this bar would have been at the end of his fist, and he wouldn't have had any contact with the women at all. As much as he'd seen as a super hero, Peter realized he had led a very sheltered life.

Ben maneuvered his way back between the crowded tables toward Peter, a Coke with ice in one hand, a bottle of beer in the other. He placed the drinks on the table, then sat down in the other chair. "Good news. The two people I was looking for are both here. Drink up. Sooner or later they'll be over to say hello."

A woman stopped by their table. She wore a low-cut blouse and had her long hair pinned atop her head. "You all set here?"

Ben smiled up at her. "For the minute. We'll be needing more."

"Then I'll be back." She sauntered away.

Peter was surprised. "There's a waitress?"

"Of course." Ben took a swig of his beer. "What kind of a low-class place did you think I brought you to? I went to get the drinks myself so I could take a look around. That's how I found the two gentlemen who will be joining us."

He stretched out in his chair. "A lot of my best stories start in places like this. Whether you live on Central Park West or in a Bowery homeless shelter, people like to talk." He waved at someone across the bar. "Here they come already. If anyone knows about Michael Luce, it'll be these two. I like speedy results."

Two men walked solemnly toward the table. One was a short black man with a mustache, the other a broad-shouldered white man with a shaved head hidden under a wool cap.

"Peter," Ben said as the two reached the table, "I'd like you to meet Turk and Grotto, two of the nicest fellows I ever found, at least when I was looking under rocks."

Turk, the black one, allowed the slightest of smiles. Grotto had no expression whatsoever. It was obvious they were a little uncomfortable with Peter around.

Turk pointed his thumb Peter's way. "So what's his story?"

"Why don't you get a couple of chairs and sit?" Ben replied. When the two of them had scrounged up a pair of seats from the surrounding tables, he added, "Peter's got a problem that I bet both of you can relate to." He clapped Peter on the arm. "Lately, the police have shown a bit too healthy an interest in him. How long were you at the station, Peter?"

Peter shrugged. "Five hours, I guess."

Grotto snorted. "Lucky they didn't keep you overnight."

"They couldn't," Ben said. "The cops didn't really have enough to hold him. And they knew I knew what was going on."

Turk nodded. "Power of the press."

"But we think the cops are going to ask him back for more," Ben continued. "And we were also thinking he could probably lead a more productive life if we could find out a few things ourselves."

"Life's always better without the cops," Grotto dead-panned.

"So who grilled you?" Turk asked.

Peter never imagined he would be the one answering questions. Ben nodded to him.

"Two guys," Peter replied. "Briscoe and Logan."

Turk whistled. "Briscoe and Logan?"

"This guy deserves a drink," Grotto said, cracking a smile at last. "Of course, Urich is paying."

Both of them found that very funny.

Peter realized that Ben knew his way around here in more ways than one. In only a minute or two, Peter had gone from being an outsider to one of the boys.

"So what say I buy a round?" Ben asked. He waved for the waitress to return.

"I guess we could go along with that," Turk allowed. "So you said you had a couple of questions?"

"Yeah, I was wondering if you boys knew anything about Michael Luce?"

Turk and Grotto looked at each other as the waitress appeared and took their order: a beer for Grotto, whiskey for Turk.

"So you want to talk about the Slickster?" Turk asked after the waitress had gone. "Nice guy—or used t'be, anyhow. Guy had vision, I'll give him that."

Grotto shook his head. "We ain't heard much about old Michael in a coupla years."

" 'Less, of course, you read the papers," Turk added.

"Shame he died, and all."

"Couldn't happen to a nicer guy."

"Mr. High-and-Mighty Michael Luce," Grotto sneered. "He came down quick enough, didn't he?"

"Wouldn't drink with folks like us anymore. Wouldn't

even acknowledge us on the street. Pretended he'd never been in places like old Josie's."

Turk spat on the floor. From the look of the linoleum, it appeared a lot of other folks had done the same.

"So was he connected?" Ben prompted.

"Was he connected?" Turk looked up at the ceiling. "Is the sky blue? You didn't hear this from me, but he used to work for Manfredi."

"Silvermane?" Peter blurted out.

Grotto scowled at him, then said to Ben, "Tell your pal t'keep it down. We try not to use that name in here."

"But back to Luce?" Ben suggested.

"Wasn't surprised he hooked up with Stewart." Grotto scowled at everyone. "Like always ends up with like."

Turk leaned toward the middle of the table. "Stewart's puttin' together an operation that'll make Manfredi seem like small potatoes. But you didn't hear that here."

Grotto pushed his empty bottle away and belched. "How about another beer, for old times' sake?"

Turk looked around. "Uh-oh. Here comes the new king of Broadway."

A young black man had entered the bar. He seemed to have something to say to everybody. "Hey, Joey! How's it going? Sammy! Seen your sister lately? Last night she said to say hello, after she said a few other things!" He laughed. "Rhonda. Why don't you return my calls? I still got two hours free on Saturday; I could pencil you in!"

He looked like he was going to trash-talk his way across the entire room; like he was on top of the world.

Grotto laughed. "Fast Anthony Davis. Fast with his money, fast with his mouth."

Ben grinned, shaking his head. "Does he ever shut up?"

Turk smiled over at Ben. "Things turned around for him lately. Anthony's got the goose that laid the golden egg—'ccordin' to Anthony, leastaways."

Peter started. He had thought this "Fast Anthony" had looked familiar from the moment he had walked in the bar, but with so little light, he couldn't be certain until Davis got fairly close. But there was no mistaking him. Davis was the man who had been with Electro at the break-in at the Department of Water and Power.

"Electro," Peter murmured.

Turk nodded. "You heard about that too? Davis had been doing odds and ends for the electric man, but that's old news. Word is Fast Anthony's working for Stewart now."

Peter sat up straight. Ben glanced at him and raised a single eyebrow. Peter knew they were both thinking the same thing. Maybe this was the man who could tell them about Luce's more recent activity. And this Electro-Stewart connection. Had Davis left one for the other, or was he working for both?

Ben pushed his chair away from the table. "This was very interesting. You fellows know where to reach me if you find out any more. Let me buy you a couple more." He threw a twenty down on the table.

"Leaving so soon?" Turk asked.

Ben nodded at Davis. "I think we'll try to talk to your Fast Anthony."

"He'll never talk to you," Grotto said. "He works for Stewart."

Turk shook his head. "Nobody who works for Stewart ever talks. They know they'll wind up dead."

"Yeah, but he's never tried not to talk to Ben Urich." Ben laughed as he stood up. "One way or another, he'll tell us what we need to know."

Fast Anthony had turned suddenly, and was walking back out the door.

"It's almost like he heard me," Ben said. "Come on, Peter. We don't want to lose him."

Peter got up and they moved quickly to the front door. They stepped out into the street. It was deserted.

"Where did he go?" Peter asked with a frown.

"I guess that's why they call him Fast Anthony," Ben replied.

We can't lose him now! Peter thought angrily. Davis could hold the key to everything.

Ben looked up and down the street. "He'd probably head back toward Second Avenue if he wanted to catch a cab—or a subway. I think we should head that way too."

Peter was afraid they had already lost him. Which was too bad. Not only was he a link to Stewart and Luce, but this was probably the only way Spider-Man was going to find Electro before the villain made his big play.

Well, where Ben and Peter couldn't follow, Spider-Man could.

"You follow him, Ben," Peter called. "I've got to make a call. I'll catch up with you later." He trotted around the corner before the reporter could say a word.

He heard Ben shout after him: "Peter? Where the hell did you go? This isn't the best neighborhood, you know!"

Ben would be surprised how well Peter knew this neighborhood, not the bars so much as the back alleys and rooftops. He could hear Ben call Peter's name a couple more times, then swear softly as he headed for Second Avenue himself.

A minute later, Peter Parker was still nowhere to be seen. But Spider-Man was sailing overhead.

He found Davis walking quickly two blocks away. Ben was right; he was headed for the F train stop on Second Avenue, all alone, the street as deserted as the one in front of the bar.

It was simplicity itself for Spider-Man to swing down and grab him from behind. Before Fast Anthony knew what had happened, he was facing Spider-Man on a rooftop.

"What did you do that for?" Davis demanded as soon as his feet were back on something solid.

"Mr. Davis," Spider-Man replied quietly. "Now we have a private place to talk."

"You know who I am, huh?" Davis looked around the rooftop. What was he looking for? A way to escape? "You better watch out. Everybody's looking for you. The word's out: you tell the cops how to find Spidey, maybe they'll do something for you in return."

This was getting off on the wrong foot. He didn't want this particular interview to be about him.

"If what you say is true, then we don't have time to fool around." He took a step toward Davis. "The time for small talk is over."

"You wouldn't do anything." Davis shook his head. "You're a hero!"

He remembered how Ben had used Peter Parker's new outlaw status back in the bar. Maybe he could do the same for Spidey's new notoriety. "Well, I used to be a hero, before that photo. Now there's a wanted poster on the front page of the *Daily Bugle*. What more do I have to lose?"

He took a single step toward Fast Anthony.

Davis threw his hands in front of his face. "Okay, so I'm sorry I took the photo!"

Spider-Man stopped. Davis had taken the photo?

"Stewart made me do it!"

Spider-Man regarded the cowering Davis for minute. "And he made you deliver it to the *Bugle,* too?"

Fast Anthony put down his hands. "Well—uh—yeah." The apologetic smile said that even Davis couldn't believe how lame his story was. "Stewart can be pretty persuasive.

He's got this guy, Andy, who would stab you as easily as he'd say hello."

Fast Anthony seemed to be relaxing. Spider-Man didn't want Davis to get too much of his confidence back. He picked up a piece of tar from the crumbling roof and held out his hand toward Davis.

"I've heard you're a clever guy." He closed his fist over the tar. "I think you might have had a hand in planning that whole thing with Luce, too."

He opened his hand and let the coal dust fall to the roof below.

Davis shook his head violently. "Hey, I didn't have anything to do with killing anybody. I find out things and people pay me. I don't use violence; I use my brain."

Luckily, he liked to talk, too. Spidey had already found more out in a couple minutes than he could have possibly hoped for. If he could keep Davis talking, maybe he could figure out how everything—Stewart, Electro, the death of Luce—fit together.

"I need the truth, Davis, about Luce and other things. You say we don't have much time. I could find some way to persuade you."

He shot out a thin strand of webbing. It wrapped itself around Fast Anthony's wrist.

Davis yelped and looked over his shoulder to see how close he was to the edge of the roof. "Man, I've already told you too much."

"You see how easy it would be for me to tie you up?"

Davis looked at the webbing stuck around his wrist. He did not look happy.

"I could hang you over the side of a building for a while until you decide to tell the truth," Spidey mused. "Nothing to worry about. My webbing doesn't dissolve for an hour or so."

Well, he might as well find out if what Turk and Grotto told him was true, too. "Besides, what's all this Stewart stuff? I thought you worked for Electro."

Davis grinned. "Come on, man. Working for a walking lightbulb? Where's the future in that?"

Spider-Man shot another strand of webbing to wrap around Davis's other wrist.

"Sure, I string Electro along!" Davis added hurriedly. "But Stewart's the future!"

This was the key. Fast Anthony was the man who could prove Spidey's innocence, and get him inside information on both Electro and Stewart. All Spidey had to do was get Davis to Ben Urich, and get the criminal to tell his story, and Spider-Man would be in the clear.

"So why don't you tell me everything Stewart's got planned?"

Davis looked doubtful again. "Man, that's like signing my own death certificate. If Stewart ever found out who—"

"What?" Spider-Man's head snapped back.

"What was that?" Davis asked. "Man, you look like somebody just whopped you on the side of the head."

It felt pretty close to that. His spider-sense was going crazy.

Davis shook his head as he looked in the air above Spidey. "I think we're both in trouble now."

A voice boomed overhead as a spotlight found Spidey. "Freeze, Spider-Man. We have you surrounded. Make it easy on all of us and give yourself up."

Spidey grabbed Davis and leaped from the spotlight's beam.

"I told you, Spidey," Davis said almost apologetically. "The cops are on your tail, and they're offering enough that the local snitches would turn in their own mother. You don't have a chance in this town."

The searchlight found him again.

"Spider-Man!" the voice boomed. "Freeze or else!"

A police helicopter swooped down overhead, a sniper's rifle pointed directly at him.

Fourteen

Mary Jane was finding this all very frustrating. She and Betty Brant had sat down in the *Bugle* building, looking through the morgue for articles on Stewart and Luce, and any connection between the two.

She was covering Stewart while Betty researched Luce. Betty was having trouble finding much of anything on the mysterious political consultant. Mary Jane, on the other hand, was finding article after article on "Mr. Money," all of them glowing with praise.

She looked up at Betty, who was at the workstation next to hers. "So why hasn't Tyler Stewart been nominated for sainthood?"

"That good, huh?" Betty laughed.

"Look at this stuff!" She had printed out some of the

earlier articles on Stewart, but had gotten more selective as the mentions began to show up almost daily. She still had a pile of twenty or thirty Stewart stories.

The files at the *Daily Bugle* were incredible. She had already accessed hundreds of pictures of Stewart at charitable events, talking about how his projects were good for the city, his use of minority construction companies, greeting children at a hospital, even adopting a dog at the pound.

She grabbed about half the printouts and handed them to Betty. "Take a look at these."

"Wow," Betty remarked as she flipped through the stories. "I work for this paper, and I had no idea we had this much on Stewart. As far as publicity is concerned, he's like Michael Jackson and Reed Richards rolled into one."

Mary Jane wondered if this really told them anything. "So I guess we now know Stewart's a publicity hound."

Betty nodded. "There's too much of it, actually. Our Tyler Stewart is a man obsessed with his image."

Mary Jane saw what she was getting at. "Which means he has something to hide?"

"Maybe, but that in itself doesn't tie him to any shady dealings." Betty did some selective reading through a couple of the articles. "It's possible he was just cruel to his mother as a child and is spending his entire life trying to atone. But I bet the real answer is much more prosaic."

"So maybe," Mary Jane mused, "he wants to look nice in the papers so he can kill people on the side?"

"Well, that certainly would be convenient," Betty agreed. "The real answer's probably just a little more complex."

They both laughed then, more to relieve tension, Mary Jane realized, than at any actual humor in their conversation. Mary Jane took a sip of coffee. It was good not to be staring at the computer screen for a minute.

Betty regarded Mary Jane for a long moment. "I'm glad Peter found someone like you."

Mary Jane was surprised by this sudden change of topic. "That's nice of you to say."

Betty sighed. "We've known each other for a long time, and we've really never talked about this. After all, Peter and I were dating before he even met you."

"I remember," Mary Jane said. She had met Betty briefly during a visit to Peter's aunt May's house—Peter himself wasn't home at the time.

"We were never really right for each other," Betty continued. "Peter was a little younger than I was, and never seemed to want to settle down. And I was going through my own little family crises, what with my mother being sick and my brother's death.

"But I've always been very fond of Peter. There was always a sadness deep inside him, ever since the death of his uncle Ben. There was always so much I felt he could never talk about.

"But Peter has changed since he got involved with you.

Some couples are like that. You seem to both buoy him up and anchor him to the ground."

Mary Jane thought then about how happy Betty had seemed when she and her late husband had first been married. "With you and Ned—"

Betty shook her head.

"Poor Ned. We didn't exactly have the perfect relationship there toward the end. His reputation was destroyed when he was accused of being the Hobgoblin. I was so happy when Peter and Spider-Man were able to help clear his name. Sometimes, I just don't know what to think. I only know one thing: Ned's gone, and I have to move on. I've decided to do my best and put it all behind me."

Mary Jane wished she could do something, say something to make Betty less sad. At least Peter and Mary Jane had stayed together, and stayed happy, despite everything that had happened. She and her hero had been very lucky. When Betty had lost Ned, she had lost a huge piece of her life.

Betty shook her head and tried to smile. "Well, this isn't getting us any closer to finding out the secret of Michael Luce."

Mary Jane had seen some reference to Luce and printed it out, then got caught up in the next article and forgot all about it. No, it wasn't Luce. She would have told Betty about that. It had to do with the next mayor of New York City.

She quickly leafed through the remaining printouts.

"Wait a moment. I should have been looking for Timilty, too." She waved Betty over. "Look at this!"

She handed Betty a photo of Stewart shaking Timilty's hand.

"Wow," Betty agreed, "this is from back in the neighborhood days of Timilty's career, back before he even got in the mayor's office. Look, it's not just Stewart—behind him, that's Silvio Manfredi."

As soon as Betty said the name, Mary Jane recognized the silver-haired crime boss better known as Silvermane. Peter had told her a lot about Manfredi over the years when the two had fought each other. Not that she'd mention it to Betty. Sometimes, as the wife of a super hero, you had to pretend you didn't know a lot.

"Now, that's a real, old-time mobster for you," Betty added. "If Timilty was involved with someone like that way back when, who knows who he is in bed with now?" She glanced up at Mary Jane. "Timilty may have been looking for a little extra campaign financing all along— something that couldn't be traced, in exchange for certain favors."

Betty looked back at the photo of Silvermane.

"There probably isn't a more ruthless crime boss in all of New York," she explained. "I wonder if Silvermane has a hand in Stewart's business? This whole anti–super hero slant of Timilty's campaign. Then Spider-Man sticks his foot in it during that bank fiasco—"

"I'm sure Spider-Man knew what he was doing." The

words were out of Mary Jane's mouth before she could think of the ramifications.

But Betty only laughed. "I know—I'm pretty sure Spider-Man's being unfairly slammed here, too, but still, the timing of that bank thing was lousy." She thought for another minute. "Maybe we don't need Silvermane as a part of this. But this whole thing with Luce smells of a setup. It makes sense if Stewart is really pulling the strings."

"So what does this give us?" MJ asked.

"It's a step in the right direction." Betty turned back to her computer terminal. "Let's see what else we can find."

MJ went back to studying the most charitable man in New York City. They had found one possible lead out of hundreds of articles. This was long and tedious work, far more frustrating than she had imagined.

She wondered if Peter was doing any better.

Spider-Man dodged behind a chimney. The police were everywhere. There were a pair of helicopters overhead, and he spotted at least a dozen men climbing over the surrounding roofs.

"Spider-Man!" a voice boomed down from one of the copters. "Make it easy on yourself. We have you surrounded!"

This wasn't exactly working out the way he had planned.

He had had to leave Davis behind. He didn't want the one man who knew the truth to be brought down by a sniper's bullet. So he'd tried to draw the pursuit away from the other man. He'd succeeded all too well. There were two copters and dozens of cops up here, and maybe two dozen squad cars on the street below.

All he needed was a moment to slip into the shadows, to ditch this Spider-Man costume and turn back into Peter Parker.

But there were no shadows. The floodlights criss-crossed every roof he chose to cross; other lights shone up from below when he swung from one building to the next.

"Spider-Man!" the voice boomed from above. "Unless you surrender at once, I will have no choice but to instruct my men to open fire!"

He was trapped.

No!

No one could trap Spider-Man. He'd just have to be faster, and sneakier. Instead of trying to escape, he needed to attack.

He stood up tall on the rooftop, his hands above his head, as a copter swooped around above. He waited for the floodlight to sweep his way, turning his hand into the floodlight's beam. He shot a quick stream of web-fluid out, covering the face of the light. The roof was plunged into darkness.

"Where is he?" someone shouted.

"Crossing the roof to the west!" someone else shouted.

And he was, too. Spider-Man ducked low to the roof, changing his direction to the south.

"No!" he called. "I saw him trying to climb down the Avenue A side!"

"Avenue A!" someone called. "Check!"

The other helicopter, with the still-functioning flood-light, swept around to illuminate Avenue A.

Spidey, for his part, found the building's roof access and took the stairs. He changed as he ran.

A moment later, Peter Parker strolled out onto the street. There were maybe twenty cop cars on this street alone.

He recognized a brand-new crew, running into the building behind him, wearing the Code Blue riot gear. The heavy guns were here. Right now, he wouldn't want to be in Spider-Man's shoes.

Peter Parker strolled back to the subway and a meeting at the *Bugle*. Cops yelled at him and maybe a dozen other onlookers to get out of the way. "Police business!"

It would take only a minute before the cops realized Spidey had slipped through their fingers. He needed to get as far away from this place as possible.

Peter realized, as he left the noise behind, that he had barely escaped the police cordon. The trick he'd used up there probably wouldn't work again.

He had some news to share with Ben and the others, though. He hoped they might have discovered a thing or two at the *Bugle*. But would any of their information be enough to track down Davis and implicate Stewart? And he still didn't understand how Electro fit into all this.

Peter hoped they could get to the truth before things got any worse. It looked like the police wanted to bring Spider-Man down at any cost.

Until this was over, he might not be able to become Spider-Man again.

Fifteen

eter hadn't quite expected this reaction when he walked into the newsroom of the *Bugle*.

First, Mary Jane rushed across the room, right into his arms. "Oh, Peter! We were so worried about you!"

Peter hugged her back, then held her at arm's length so he could look at her. "Well, last time I checked, I was still in one piece. Did something happen here?"

"Well," MJ explained, "Ben called, and said he'd lost you. And then there were all these reports of a heavy police presence right around the area where you'd disappeared. We heard gunshots fired when we were watching the live remote. Anything could have happened!"

Peter shook his head. He wondered how much he should say with Betty in the room. "Well, a lot did happen, actually. I was going to try to call you, and then I couldn't find a working phone."

"In that neighborhood, I'm surprised you could find a phone that hadn't been ripped out of the wall," Betty said from where she sat in front of a computer terminal. "It probably wasn't too good an idea to get separated from Ben."

Now he was being lectured by both sides. It was like he was fourteen again, and both Betty and Mary Jane had suddenly turned into his aunt May. "Hey, I'm a big-time news photographer. I laugh at danger, at least sometimes. Besides, I haven't gotten killed yet."

Betty shook her head, too. "Well, I suppose I've done a foolish thing or two for the *Bugle,* too. But you said a lot happened. Like what?"

"Well, like I said, Ben and I got separated," Peter replied. "I was going to try and find him, but suddenly the streets were full of cops. They'd found Spider-Man, somewhere up on the rooftops. And when I say the streets were full of cops, I mean *full* of cops. There were squad cars, helicopters, and searchlights everywhere. And me without my camera."

Betty laughed. "Peter Parker and his one-track mind."

"Hey, a guy's gotta make a living."

Mary Jane regarded him skeptically. "That's fine, as long as a guy doesn't get himself killed doing it."

"I did manage to catch up with a guy we were following," Peter continued. "Fast Anthony Davis. I got some good stuff from him, too. From what he told me, he's worked for both Electro and Tyler Stewart. More than that, he was the one who took that photo of Spider-Man holding Luce."

It was Betty's turn to be skeptical. "Can you really believe his story?"

"Why wouldn't he believe it?" Mary Jane asked.

"Getting in the newspaper is one way to become famous," Betty replied. "You'd be amazed the lengths some people would go to to get their pictures in the paper."

"I'm pretty sure Davis knows what he's talking about," Peter said. "He had a couple of facts about Spider-Man that he couldn't have known unless he was there."

Betty grinned. "Which means you've been talking to Spider-Man since this happened? Consorting with a wanted fugitive—Peter, I'm proud of you. Think there's any way Betty Brant could get an exclusive interview with the web-slinger?"

Peter shook his head. "Spider-Man usually finds me. It rarely works the other way around. I think right now Spidey's kind of busy."

"It would be good to get his side of the story. And the *Bugle* would *have* to run it, too. Talk about newsworthy!" She smiled. "Sometimes it's fun to watch Jonah get a little hot under the collar."

Peter guessed he was glad other *Bugle* employees occasionally liked to torment their publisher, too. After all of Jameson's talk about deemphasizing Spider-Man, it would be great to put the super hero back on the front page. It was too bad that, with trying to clear Spider-Man and track down Electro—and who knew where the Rhino would strike next?—they didn't have the time.

"Besides," Peter added, "Davis is the one who delivered the incriminating photo to the *Bugle*. There should be footage of him on the security cameras, I would guess sometime between two and four A.M. That would be the clincher."

"Yeah," Betty agreed. "We might even be able to get a usable photo of Davis off the videotape. Peter, this is sounding better and better. But didn't Davis spill his guts awfully easily?"

Not when Davis was being grilled by Spider-Man. But Peter couldn't very well tell Betty that.

"He was nervous. He obviously felt that he was in over his head, and knew that if he didn't talk to me, he could end up answering to Spider-Man. It was too bad I didn't get to ask him more. He took off when there got to be too many cops."

Peter looked around the newsroom. "So where's Ben?"

"He said he had to track down a couple more leads," Betty answered. "I think he might still be out there looking for you."

Peter smiled sheepishly. "Well, if you see him before I do, tell him I'm sorry I lost him, or I guess he lost me. I'd like to talk to him. He might be able to help fill in a couple of the holes in Davis's story."

"Peter, look," MJ said. "There's a news bulletin."

All three turned to the video monitor in the corner of the newsroom, always tuned to one of the all-news stations. Mary Jane walked over and turned up the sound.

"We repeat," the announcer's voice spoke over some live pictures of a large, factorylike structure. "Electro has taken control of the New York Department of Water and Power's Yonkers pumping facility. Unless Electro's demands are met, he is threatening to completely shut off New York's water supply. The police and special Code Blue units have been called to the scene, but our most recent reports indicate that they have not been able to penetrate the electrical field Electro has managed to place around the facility.

"For the background of the man who would hold New York City hostage, let's turn to this special report from WNN correspondent Allysen Palmer."

The words FILE FOOTAGE appeared at the bottom the screen as the scene shifted to a videotape of a rooftop fight between Electro and Spider-Man.

"Electro's real name is Maxwell Dillon. Dillon was working as a lineman for Consolidated Edison when he was hit by lightning in a freak accident, turning him into what one scientist called a 'living electrical capacitor.' Electro has plagued New York City over a dozen times through the years, briefly as a member of the Sinister Six, the Frightful Four, and the Emissaries of Evil. He usually prefers to operate solo, however, as he appears to be doing in the present crisis. Evidence suggests that in recent months Electro's power has greatly increased, not good news for city authorities. As you can see from our file footage, Electro's most persistent adversary over the years has been Spider-Man, who is also now being sought by New York authorities in connection with the death of Michael Luce."

The scene shifted to a talking head. "WNN has just received the text of Electro's ransom demands to the city. I quote," the newsreader said as he looked down at a piece of paper, " 'Mr. Mayor. I now control the water supply of the entire city of New York. You have twenty-four hours to pay me one billion dollars, or New York will become a very dry place. Any additional delay on your part, and I will use my powers to damage the system in such a way that New York will be without water for a very long time to come.' "

The announcer paused for a moment, then nodded at the camera. "We now take you to City Hall, and Deputy Mayor Barbara Barron."

The scene shifted again to a podium, behind which stood a thin woman with dark hair and a dark business suit.

"Gentlemen and ladies of the press," the deputy mayor began. "I have a prepared statement from the mayor." She looked down at a paper before her.

"At this point in time," she read, "we have entered preliminary talks with Electro to obtain the release of the pumping station in Yonkers. While there are no easy answers in a situation like this, we would like to assure the people of the city that we will do our utmost to keep this unfortunate incident from interfering with their daily lives.

"The mayor and the people of New York do not approve of someone dictating terms over something as precious as this city's water supply. Should we manage to negotiate a settlement with Electro on this matter, any money that might change hands would have to be approved by the proper chain of command within the city and the state, and then assembled and transported to whatever point might be mutually agreed upon. Even in the event of the two parties reaching a mutual understanding, it will therefore take us far longer than the original twenty-four-hour deadline presented to the city. Therefore, the mayor's first priority will be to get Electro to extend his deadline so that both sides might negotiate in good faith. Thank you."

The deputy mayor turned and walked away from the podium, ignoring the reporters' shouted questions.

"Sounds like a delaying tactic to me," Betty commented. "The mayor's office really only said two things in that statement: they've agreed to talk, and they want more time."

The bulletin had returned to the news studio.

"And now," a voiceover announced, "a WNN exclusive!"

The camera showed a two-shot of the station's prime female anchor next to Brian Timilty, who looked very well groomed for this early in the morning.

"New York City mayoral candidate Brian Timilty has been nice enough to come down to our studio," the anchor announced, "so that he might respond to the mayor's statement in person." She turned and smiled at her guest. "Mr. Timilty. Glad you could make it so early in the morning."

"Glad to be here, Wannetta. As soon as my aides informed me of this crisis, I knew I needed to be involved, as would anybody who cares about the future of New York City."

"So you have heard the mayor's statement?" Wannetta asked.

"Yes, I have."

"And what is your initial reaction?"

Timilty turned and frowned directly at the camera.

"I believe the mayor is at the very least misguided. We cannot negotiate with costumed terrorists. I think an incident like this shows the truth in what I have been saying all along. Letting these crazed vigilantes run loose in New York will only bring ruin on our fair city."

"So you'd place Electro in the same category as someone like Spider-Man?"

"Who wouldn't? Now, with the murder of my campaign manager, Michael Luce, Spider-Man's true motives have become apparent. He and all the other costumed lunatics are in this for their own glory, with the good people of New York as their innocent victims."

Peter had to stay calm. It didn't matter what Timilty or anybody said, as long as he found a way to clear Spider-

Man's name. This was all falling into place. The current mayor of New York was in a no-win situation. Either he "negotiated with costumed terrorists," or he allowed the city's water supply to be crippled, something that might lead to everything from billions of dollars in lost revenues to riots in the street. Through it all, Timilty could take the high ground, letting the mayor do all the dirty work.

And the net result? Electro gets the money, Stewart gets Timilty elected so that he can control the city, and Spider-Man ends up as the "costumed vigilante" fall guy.

"Isn't it awfully convenient that Timilty was able to reach the news studio only moments after Electro released his demands?" Betty mused. "One could almost imagine Timilty somehow got advance word of Electro's plans."

"It certainly is beginning to look like that," Mary Jane agreed. "At least to us here in the room. It's too bad you can't come up with some hard evidence to back up the story."

"Never say can't," Betty said with a frown. "There's got to be a way."

"I think so, too," Peter agreed. "I may need to go out again and check something out. But first I need to do a little research."

"This computer's mine!" Betty called. "You go and get your own."

Peter grinned at her attempt at humor and walked over to the terminal next to the pair Betty and Mary Jane were already using.

He had a couple of ideas he quickly needed to check out. If he was right, he could at least take care of Electro.

I hear you knockin', but you can't come in.

Electro threw back his head and laughed as he thought of the lyrics to that old rock-and-roll song. All of New York City wanted to come in to this pumping station, but they could knock and knock and not get anywhere. Electro had them in an electrical lockout. By the time they figured out a way through the force field, he'd have the money and be gone. A billion dollars could keep him in Rio de Janeiro for a long time.

He looked back at the monitor installed above the gleaming silver control board. He had never found television so entertaining, and on the all-news station, too! Electro just couldn't get enough of it.

He loved the constant shots of police cars, helicopters, riot vehicles, even a couple of items of heavy artillery that they seemed to have borrowed from the Army. They would try anything and everything to try to blast his electrical shield. Nothing would get through, though. Of course, they didn't want to hurt their precious pumping station. If they were too heavy-handed with the firepower, they could shut down the city without any help from Electro.

All the major roads out of New York were clogged with traffic, people fleeing the chaos they expected would come once the city had been turned into a desert. It was the sort of thing you'd see down south with hurricane warnings.

Hurricanes and Electro; he liked the comparison. He had always wanted to be a force of nature.

But what was a victory worth if it couldn't be shared? Sure, there was the one technician who had been on duty when Electro had walked in to take over. A slight shock had knocked the man unconscious long enough for him to get properly trussed up. Electro didn't believe in taking unnecessary chances. It was always good to have someone around who knew the system in case something went wrong.

He decided he needed to share his victory, and check on the backup plan. By now, Fast Anthony should have set the special charges for the old unused tunnels two miles to the west. While not as large as the Yonkers power plant, the older pipes were another way to get upstate water down to the city. With the opening of the ultramodern Yonkers plant that Electro had now commandeered, the old pipes and tunnels had been considered redundant, and shut down by cost-cutting measures. Not maintained for the past couple of years, they could probably still carry water into New York City while repairs were made to the Yonkers plant; unless, of course, a tragic accident happened when the water hit the unused tunnels.

It was Davis's job to arrange that accident. As soon as Electro had secured the Yonkers pumping station, his henchman had gone with a pair of Stewart's men to rig the tunnels with plastic explosives.

If the city didn't discover the old tunnels, or decided

not to use them, nothing would happen. But if they tried to bypass the Yonkers facility, and reuse the old system, the weight of the water would set off the plastic explosives, causing the tunnels to collapse, and giving the city no choice but to bargain with Electro.

Electro hoped the city tried to use the old system. He wanted to see the look on their faces when they failed. He imagined how dramatic the shots of the rushing water would look on the all-news station, flooding out homes, washing out roads, and getting nowhere at all near New York City.

He decided to call Fast Anthony and see how his end of the plan was going.

There was no answer. Electro was being too impatient. Davis must still be setting things up in the tunnels, and so would still be out of reach of his cell phone.

At least he hoped that's what it meant. They should have arranged some signal beforehand. But Davis was quick and clever, and they had the resources of Tyler Stewart to fall back on now. Between the two, they should be able to overcome any problem.

Electro wasn't used to waiting. He would much rather be on a rooftop somewhere locked in a life-and-death struggle with Spider-Man than stuck in a chair watching the news. But now that he had secured the pumping station, there was nothing left to do but wait.

He just needed every angle covered.

If Fast Anthony was unavailable, he would call Tyler Stewart instead. He picked up the phone and dialed.

"You've reached the boss," a man's voice said.

"Electro here. I need to talk to Stew—"

"No names, please," the voice on the other end of the line cut him off. "All calls to this number are scrambled, but you can't be too careful. I'll put the boss on."

Electro waited through a few seconds of annoying Muzak.

"Congratulations," Stewart chuckled on the other end of the line. "You are now the most important man in New York."

Electro hadn't exactly thought of it that way. "I guess I am, huh?"

"What could be as dramatic as holding all of New York for ransom? I have to admit it, Electro, you've got style!"

Yeah, that was exactly what he was feeling. "Thanks," he said. "But this is business. I haven't got any word from my man Davis about the backup plan. I was wondering if you've been in touch with your men on that."

"No," Stewart replied. "I haven't heard from them. I wouldn't worry yet; it's still pretty early in the game. I'll check and see if there was a problem."

Electro liked the businessman's no-nonsense approach. Maybe Stewart was worth that ten percent after all.

"My guess is that," Stewart added, "in the next few hours, everything will fall into place. Hang on a minute."

Electro got to hear another few seconds of Muzak.

"I've got to go," Stewart said as soon as he got back on the line. "Hang in there. One way or another, I know Electro will be paid in full."

Electro hung up the phone and looked back to the monitors. They showed the hillside immediately outside the pumping station, where a dozen or so cops in Code Blue combat gear were slowly advancing on the fence Electro had used to help generate the protective field he'd thrown around the facility. Most of the Code Blue people were carrying what looked like some sort of futuristic guns. These guys were famous for their anti–super-power gizmos. Some of that stuff might even be able to penetrate the electrical field he'd set up around this place—unless, of course, someone was there to regenerate the field and blast any of the gizmos they wanted to use against him.

Electro got up from his chair and stretched. Sparks danced at the ends of his fingers. At least this little confrontation would give him something to do.

Peter decided this really was a brave new world.

Everything, it seemed, was on the Internet, if you only knew where to look. He could access plans for all city projects, including copies of the basic construction blueprints, or anything else that by law had to be available for public scrutiny. A few things such as the actual design of the pumps would probably be classified, to prevent the sort of terrorist action that Electro had just begun. But the basic public buildings and tunnels were all here somewhere, if you could figure out where to look.

It wasn't hard to access maps of underground New York City. But there were thousands of miles of tunnels beneath greater New York, not just for water, but electricity, gas, waste disposal, automobile traffic, and the extensive system of subways and commuter trains. As Spider-Man, he had explored some of those tunnels. It had taken him a good ten minutes to locate the water system around the Yonkers pumping station. Now he had to look through the subsystems around the station, and the actual plans for the pumping station itself.

WNN was reporting on a confrontation between Electro and the elite Code Blue forces. So far, it seemed to have generated a lot of electrical sparks and no tangible results. Despite Code Blue's best efforts, Electro's force field was holding.

He'd let Electro and Code Blue duke it out for a while longer. He had to see if there was another way into the master control room, or maybe a way to divert the water around the pumping station, some way to get Electro's hands off the controls long enough so that Spider-Man could take him out for good.

Wait a minute. Here was an auxiliary station, no longer used, where they might be able to divert enough water to keep New York from going bone dry. Peter quickly printed copies of the area maps, as well as the building plans for the pumping station. It appeared there were a pair of emergency pipes, used only for runoff if the water level got too high—not too likely considering what little rain New York had received in the past couple of months. These might be the perfect entrance for Spider-Man.

"Betty!" he called. "I think I've got something here." He quickly explained about how he saw a way to divert the water around the main pumping station. He decided to keep the information about the alternate ways into the pumping station to himself.

"Great," Betty said. "We should make some calls and check into that."

"That's what I like to see, reporters on a story even before I get here."

Robbie Robertson walked in the door, trailed by another of the *Bugle*'s reporters, Joy Mercado.

The editor headed straight for Peter. "Peter. Good, I'm glad you're here. We need a photographer to go up to Yonkers with Joy and cover what's going on at the pumping station."

Peter nodded. "We're on it."

In a way, this was ideal. As Peter Parker, he could scope out the whole situation at the pumping station, without having to avoid any of the police. Then, as long as his new information was correct, he could quietly slip away and let Spider-Man confront Electro. He'd worked with Joy before, and she knew he liked to go off on his own to get the best possible camera angle.

Mary Jane gave him a quick hug. "You be careful."

Peter grinned and shrugged. "I always bring the photos back. Otherwise, I don't get paid."

There had to be some way to stop Electro. He hoped the access tunnels were close enough to the pumping station for him to locate them aboveground, and far enough away from the action for Spider-Man to access them undetected. Whatever plan he hit upon, he had less than twenty-four hours to make it work.

Robbie glanced over at Betty. "And what are you working on?"

"Give me another couple of hours, Robbie," Betty replied, "and I'm going to give you a story you won't believe."

Maybe they could even clear Spider-Man's name while they were at it. The way things had been going, Peter doubted it.

First he had to save New York City. Then he could worry about the small stuff like his reputation.

"There!" Betty announced. "That has to be him."

Mary Jane looked over Betty's shoulder at the frozen video image from the *Bugle*'s lobby security camera. It showed a young, black male, perhaps in his early twenties, dressed in black jeans, black T-shirt, black leather jacket, and mirrorshades despite the late hour.

"Let's see how far the camera follows him." She slow-motioned the tape forward.

The stranger walked up to the security station in the

lobby. The guard seemed half asleep. The stranger and the guard exchanged a few words. The guard laughed and waved him right through. So much for the *Bugle*'s security.

This, apparently, was "Fast Anthony" Davis. When he was in front of the security guard he looked like he could handle himself just about anywhere, but as soon as he walked past the security station, Mary Jane could see there was an underlying nervousness in the way he looked around the empty corridor and felt for the package in his pocket—twice; no, three times—as if he was doing something not quite legal.

He stepped into the elevator and out of camera range.

"It sure looks like Davis to me." She rewound the tape slightly. "There was one point when he looked almost directly at the camera. I'll capture the image here and print it out. That way, we'll have something to show people."

Mary Jane frowned. She was missing something here.

"We'll have something to show? What are you talking about?"

"The police want Spider-Man one way or another. Peter stayed out of jail the first time they questioned him, mostly because he was a member of the press. If the police can't get Spider-Man soon, they'll bring Peter back in, and this time I think they'll hold him for a while. At the very least, Peter is a material witness. With his ongoing relationship with Spider-Man, the police may even charge him as an accomplice."

"How could they do something like that?"

"They could do anything. This, after all, is an election year, and thanks to our friend Timilty, super heroes are a hot topic."

So the cops are going to arrest either Spider-Man or Peter Parker? MJ thought despairingly. Either way, they lost.

"What can we do?" Mary Jane asked.

"We have to clear Spider-Man's name. And to do that, I think we need to find Mr. Anthony Davis."

"Find Anthony Davis? How?"

"Hey," Betty answered as she grabbed her purse, "Ben Urich isn't the only reporter with connections in this town."

Betty must know what she's doing. Mary Jane followed her out the door. But why did MJ keep thinking about that conversation they'd had an hour or so ago, about all the crazy things Peter and Betty had done for the *Daily Bugle*?

Sixteen

Fast Anthony was going to have to be faster than he had ever been in the past. Six hours before, he had been sure nothing could go wrong. Now he just wanted to get out of the way before everything started to fall apart.

He had almost forgotten one of the prime rules of the street. You always had to cover your butt, especially when you were working for two bosses. But what happened when the bosses disagreed, and started to change each other's plans?

The plan had been quite specific. There was another upstate pumping station that could take over sixty percent of the water flow from the Yonkers plant. The reduction might still cause some problems for the city of New York, but it reduced Electro's threat from a catastrophe to an inconvenience. Davis was to go to the old pumping station with Tom Devlin and Andy to lay explosives that would detonate if any water passed through the pipes.

Davis left Electro at the Yonkers plant, then returned to the city to meet with Stewart's men. It was only then that he learned about the change of plan. Devlin let him know that he was no longer needed. Devlin and Andy would do the job without him. Through it all, Andy played with his switchblade and giggled. The implication was that if he had any objection, he would shortly be dead.

The final insult was when Tom Devlin asked Fast Anthony for his cell phone. Andy had stepped behind Davis as Devlin had held out his hand. All Davis could remember was how loud Andy's high-pitched giggle sounded that close to his ear. He handed over the phone, his only link with Electro. Then Devlin and Andy took off in Stewart's car, leaving Davis alone on the street and totally out of the loop.

For the first time in his life, Fast Anthony had no idea what to do. There was no phone number for the Yonkers pumping facility. There was probably some way to get through to it from the Department of Water and Power's central switchboard, but Davis doubted that would work while the place was being held hostage. So Davis had been left behind with no way to contact Electro, and nothing to do but sit on his hands. At the very least, he would be cut out of a lucrative job in Stewart's organization. At the very worst, Electro and he were being double-crossed.

And Davis had a very bad feeling that this wasn't the

end of it. When this job was all over, Andy might be coming around to take care of him anyway.

Fast Anthony Davis felt his world crumbling beneath his feet. He had always figured that if he kept himself useful enough to Electro, that would keep him safe. But now, with the electric guy barricaded in a pumping station in Yonkers, anything could happen.

Well, he was doubly glad now that he'd managed to take that little bit of insurance back at the murder scene. The way things were going now, the safest place for Fast Anthony Davis might be in the arms of the law.

To Peter Parker, the Yonkers pumping station looked less like a major source of water than it did a circus.

He and Joy had gotten up here in one of the *Bugle* staff cars, mostly by taking back roads in the Bronx. Luckily, Joy knew her way around the northernmost borough—Peter had been introduced to sections of the Bronx he never knew existed. The main traffic arteries out of town were already clogged with people, all going in the opposite direction from the usual morning commute. If Electro did nothing else, he had already scared a large percentage of New Yorkers into getting out of town.

Even though very little had happened at the pumping station after Electro's takeover, Peter and Joy were getting there a little late in the game. Both the police—with units from New York City, Yonkers, the state, and Code Blue—and other members of the press had had plenty of time to set up camp. Peter saw seven different news vans, and maybe half as many cop cars as had been following Spider-Man the day before, including three of the specially marked Code Blue vans. And everybody—press, police, blue-suited commandos—was doing nothing but waiting.

If Spider-Man showed up here, he'd be overwhelmed by cops looking for something to do. If he was going to get inside the pumping station, he'd have to start his journey as Peter Parker.

Joy Mercado parked at the edge of the carnival. There were so many cars in front of them, it was probably still a good ten-minute walk to the fenced-in pumping station.

She frowned, pushing her blond hair off her forehead. "This doesn't exactly look like the best place to get an exclusive." She sighed as she grabbed a notebook and tape recorder.

"Oh, well." She opened the driver's-side door. "Follow me. Maybe you can get a good, low-angle shot of Electro or something."

Peter heard another set of car doors slam shut behind them. He turned to look at the next car as he climbed out. "I think we've got another exclusive," he called to Joy. "Look who just pulled in behind us."

"That's what you need a photographer for," Joy said with a wolfish grin. "They tend to see things."

Candidate for mayor Brian Timilty and a young woman, probably Luce's replacement, were walking right toward them.

Joy was in his face in a matter of seconds. "Mr. Timilty. What brings you to Yonkers?"

Publicity and a photo opportunity, Peter thought. He dutifully focused his camera, walking around to the side so that he could get both Timilty and the still-distant power station in the same shot.

Timilty frowned at the reporter. He turned slightly so that Peter would get a full-face shot of him rather than a profile. "As you know, for much of my career I worked in the mayor's office. I was personally involved in the development of this pumping station for the city's water supply. Because of this, I have some valuable information about the station that I think the police need to know."

Peter looked up from the camera. "Excuse me for interrupting, Joy. Mr. Timilty, are you talking about those unused tunnels that might be used to divert the water?"

Joy gave Peter a *how did you know that?* look. Even Timilty looked a little flustered.

"Well, yes, Mr. Parker, isn't it? That is one of the options I want to talk about with the men in charge here. Thanks to my past involvement with this project, I know the tunnels. I know the equipment. I thought it would be best if I came out here personally to lend a hand." He nodded pleasantly to Joy Mercado. "Now, if you'll excuse me, time is short."

He and his assistant turned away and walked quickly toward the mass of police and reporters farther down the road.

"Peter," Joy said as soon as the two were out of earshot. "Sometimes you amaze me. How did you know about the other tunnels?"

"It was one of the things Betty and I discovered when we were researching the city's water system. It's interesting that Timilty has such an intimate knowledge of the project."

"You think it's too convenient?" Joy smiled. "Maybe Timilty's in league with Electro, and they're going to split the money. Peter, you've been reading too many conspiracy books. But this is a great story. I'm going to give Robbie a quick call and let him know about it, then go in and see if he drops any other bombshells when he talks to the rest of the press."

"Fine," Peter agreed. "I'll try to get in closer to the action, maybe get a picture of Timilty near the fence. Maybe I can get a shot of Electro and Timilty together."

"Sounds good. If we can't find each other in that madhouse up there, what say we rendezvous back at the car"— she glanced at her watch—"say in an hour?"

"Sounds good to me," Peter agreed. "Between us, we'll get at the truth."

"Or at least we'll get some good Brian Timilty sound bites." She waved to Peter as she pulled out her cell phone.

Peter turned away and jogged toward the pumping station. A crowd of well over a hundred people had clustered around the gate of the facility, most of them staring at the station—or, more accurately, at the field of electricity that surrounded the station. As Peter remembered the map, the closer of the two access tunnels to the station would be located to his right, at the bottom of the hill. A couple of the cops were walking the perimeter of the fence; everybody else seemed content to cram into the smallest space possible. He could walk casually around the pumping station on the pretext of finding the best possible shot, and probably not see more than one or two others outside of the gate area.

Somebody was shouting up ahead. Peter looked to the crowd, half expecting some new light show from Electro. But it was just the first few reporters noticing the approach of Brian Timilty. Two dozen people turned away from the gate and ran down the road toward the mayoral candidate.

Well, Peter thought, *two distractions for the price of one.* He could think of no better time to slip off and become Spider-Man.

Electro felt like the walls were closing in on him. Bright stainless steel and concrete that seemed to reflect every light in the place, every flashing bulb and glowing dial beating down on him, pressing against him, crushing him into an ever-smaller space.

Where was Davis? Stewart had supplied him with a car and a cell phone that was supposed to speed dial straight to Electro so that Fast Anthony could continue to be Electro's eyes and ears to the outside world. Once Davis had placed the explosives, he was supposed to call in his success with the code words *The power's off.* Then he would station himself outside the Yonkers pumping station in case there was some last-minute change of plan.

The whole thing had seemed so clean and simple, especially with the backing of Stewart's people and resources. Now it felt like nothing so much as a simple disaster. Something had happened to Davis, or his phone, and Electro was cut off from the outside world.

Well, he wasn't completely cut off. He could still call Tyler Stewart. And if something had gone wrong on Davis's end, Electro could get Stewart to fix it.

Electro picked up the cell phone and punched in the second speed-dial number.

"Sorry," the voice said at the other end of the line. "Boss isn't here."

"Don't give me that. Tell him I need to talk to him."

"I'll pass it on."

The other man hung up.

What did that mean? Stewart had told Electro he'd be available throughout the plan, and now this.

Something felt very wrong. Electro wanted out of here. He couldn't wait sixteen more hours for a yes or no. He'd call back the mayor and demand the money within the hour.

Speak of the devil. Electro glanced up at the television monitor, and there, on the news station, was the mayor of New York. Electro walked across the room to better hear what His Honor was saying.

"Perhaps I've been misunderstood," the mayor said to a room full of reporters. "I thought it was best to take a cautious approach and explore all the options. But it was never my intention to condone terrorism.

"Under no circumstances will we buckle under to Electro's demands. I hope that the people of New York realize that if I have ever sounded uncertain or overly conciliatory, it was in the interests of seeing that the city maintained its water supply until other plans could be put into effect."

What the hell is this? Does he think I'm bluffing? Maybe I should forget the money and trash the pumping station now. Electro wouldn't get rich, but he'd turn New York City into a ghost town. His name would be remembered forever.

The reporters were shouting questions at the mayor now.

"How do you feel about Brian Timilty being the one to bring forward the information about alternate routes for the water supply?"

The mayor nodded and smiled, although even Electro could tell that he wasn't very happy. "Mr. Timilty did what any good citizen would have done. Brought forth pertinent information in a timely manner. People in my own administration had already been researching alternate strategies for supplying the city with water, but Timilty's statement saved us precious hours of time." The mayor coughed. "I would like to personally thank Mr. Timilty for the information, and would like to assure him that, after I am re-elected mayor, I shall be proud to appoint him water commissioner."

The reporters all laughed, but Electro didn't find it at all funny.

Timilty was turning against him? But Timilty was Stewart's man. This whole blackmail scheme was going to make the mayor look like a fool and pave Timilty's way to the election. The plan would have benefited Timilty, Stewart, and Electro all at the same time.

The plan was foolproof.

What happened to Davis?

Electro pushed the speed dial one more time.

Someone picked it up on the second ring.

"Davis?" Electro shouted into the phone. "Hello?"

There was no reply.

"Davis? What's the matter with this phone?"

The connection was broken at the other end, but not before Electro heard a very familiar high-pitched giggle.

They were playing with him! Davis, Stewart, Timilty—all playing with him!

Electro looked up.

The walls were closing in.

This, supposedly, was Fast Anthony's home turf, a half run-down, half newly gentrified strip of the Lower East Side. Mary Jane wasn't entirely sure what to make of it.

Apparently, Davis had had a lot of girlfriends, young women who, by and large, were not all that happy with

Davis's lack of continuing attention, and were all too eager to talk.

"He sounds like a charming fellow," Mary Jane commented after they'd had their third almost identical interview.

"He probably is," Betty agreed, "until he gets exactly what he wants. What do we really know so far? He likes women, but he doesn't really want to be tied down. It sounds like he's never had an honest job in his life, and yet he's never gone to jail. Our Fast Anthony is not only charming, he's a survivor."

"So where do we go from here?" MJ asked.

"I think we've gotten enough of his background," Betty mused.

"Maybe too much," MJ agreed. They had started out by casing the beauty parlors in a three-block radius of Davis's home address. They had found one of his girlfriends at the second establishment they entered. At first, MJ had thought they had been extraordinarily lucky. It was only after talking to these women for a little while that she realized that Fast Anthony had had an extraordinary number of girlfriends. And every one of them was willing to name three or four other women who were responsible for their relationship's demise, as if the other women were to blame, rather than the interviewee's judgment or Fast Anthony's roving eye.

"Well, we now know things about Fast Anthony that we don't want to know," Betty continued. Two of the women had been quite frank. "And things that have no place in a family newspaper." She pulled her notebook from her purse. "But we did get a listing of his favorite haunts." She flipped a page. "What is this, Wednesday? We might be able to find him getting his hair cut."

"Every Wednesday?" MJ asked.

"Sure. You remember what—who was it?—Lenore said about his motto? 'When you got the money, you look good.' "

Both the women laughed at that. It was the odd thing about Fast Anthony; when it came to women, he was something of a jerk, but all the women who got involved with him still sounded a little wistful whenever they talked about him. MJ already felt he was charming, and she hadn't even met him.

"Here's the place," Betty announced.

She looked across the street. There was a little basement shop behind a wrought-iron fence. The sign on the fence said CHRISTOPHER'S CUTTERS.

"And look who's walking up the steps. I tell you, good reporting always pays off."

A young black male, wearing clothes identical to those caught by the *Bugle*'s security camera, bounded up the steps and turned to walk down the sidewalk.

"We've got to catch him," Betty said, running across the street. Mary Jane hurried to follow.

"Mr. Davis!" Betty called. "We need to talk with you!"

Davis spun around warily. He looked like he was ready

to start running, too. But when he saw two attractive young women rushing toward him, he straightened up and smiled.

"Ladies?" he asked.

"Mr. Davis?" Betty flashed her reporter's credentials. "We're from the *Bugle,* and we'd like to ask you a couple of questions about the murder of Michael Luce."

"Luce?" Davis's smile vanished. "I don't know any Luce. I'm afraid you have the wrong guy." He turned and quickly began to walk away.

"No we don't, Mr. Davis," Betty called as she walked after him. "We know you're the one who delivered those photos to the *Bugle.* You know the photos I'm talking about, Mr. Davis?"

Davis said something under his breath and started running.

"Oh no you don't," Betty said. Both women took off after him.

One thing about working as a model: you needed to get a lot of exercise to stay in shape. Mary Jane never realized she'd ever put all those hours on the treadmill to this particular use. She quickly dashed ahead of Betty.

Davis ducked down a side street. Mary Jane was right on his heels. He dodged down a second alley, then a third. Mary Jane was never more than twenty feet behind him. Davis zigzagged to his left toward an alley; Mary Jane kept on after him.

Peter, she kept thinking. *I have to catch him to clear Peter.*

The alley was a dead end. Davis whirled around.

"I always wanted to be chased by a pretty woman," he said with a smile. "But there's some things I just can't talk about. So let me walk out of here and there won't be any trouble."

Mary Jane shook her head no. She had to clear Peter, and Spider-Man.

"The only way you're getting out of here is after you talk to me." She had taken her share of self-defense classes. She could hold her own, one on one. Hell, one time she took down the Chameleon, one of Spider-Man's oldest foes, all by her lonesome. She could deal with this guy.

"Good-looking or not," Davis grumbled, "I'm getting tired of this." He lunged for Mary Jane.

MJ stepped nimbly out of his way. But Davis was taller than she was, with a greater reach. She needed something to even the odds.

She grabbed a garbage can lid as Davis jumped for her again. He missed her, but got the lid full in the face. He sat down hard.

"Ow!" Davis exclaimed. "That hurt! What do you want from me, anyway? I can't tell you anything."

"You don't get it, do you?" Mary Jane did her best to sneer. "Spider-Man sent us, and if we can find you this easily, what makes you think you can avoid him?"

Even though she said "we," MJ realized that Betty was nowhere around. She had lost the reporter in the process of zigzagging around after Davis.

"Oh yeah," Davis agreed, "Spider-Man." He watched MJ as he massaged his jaw. "And he's got people working for him that are every bit as crazy as he is."

"You'd better believe it," Mary Jane said. "So who killed Michael Luce?"

Davis thought about it for a moment. "Okay. Just let me walk around a minute."

MJ banged the trash can lid with her fist. "You get up and try something, you get this again."

Davis looked at MJ, as if considering his options. "Oh hell, I'm probably dead anyway." He looked up at Mary Jane. "Luce's death was arranged by a man named Tyler Stewart."

"I know who that is."

"Who doesn't?" Davis agreed. "But Luce was actually killed by one of Stewart's goons, a guy named Andy."

"Can you prove this?" Mary Jane demanded.

"Of course I can prove it. I always cover my rear. I took the photos of Spider-Man and Luce that showed up in the *Bugle*. But I took another roll of photos, too. I had one of those little disposable cameras. The kind you can get in a drugstore?"

Really? Mary Jane thought. *Now, this sounds promising.*

"And what was on that roll?"

Davis smiled. "Shots of the guy who really did the killing."

Seventeen

Spider-Man had come too far to lose it all now.

Timilty had proved to be an excellent distraction. First the press flocked around him, then most of the police came over to see what was going on. Peter Parker could have driven a truck through the area and no one would have noticed. So it was a piece of cake for him to quickly head down the hill and slip into the drainage tunnel, and into his costume, unnoticed.

It was a shame the rest of his trip wasn't as easy. Fifty feet into the tunnel, he found his way blocked by a heavy metal grate, probably to keep stray animals from doing the same thing he was. It took a full minute and all of his spider-strength to pull the grating loose. Once he passed that obstacle, he walked another fifty feet and found that his tunnel broke off into three smaller pipes, each still large enough to crawl through. He had to consult the printout of the map, which told him the pipe on the right was his best bet. After about fifty feet, that opened up into another six-foot-high tunnel, which again split off in three directions.

Down here, the tunnels were a hopeless maze and the map was more or less useless. He picked the central tunnel this time, and kept on walking, trusting that he was going in the right general direction.

These interior tunnels are filled with large pools of standing water, he thought. *And water is a great conductor.* With all the moisture down here, he hoped the electrical current was restricted to the surface.

The tunnel sloped upward ahead. Spidey crossed his fingers. Maybe there was a way out of here after all.

Electro couldn't stand it anymore. He was going to trash the place. Sure, destroying the pumping station would cost him a billion dollars, but, frankly, that billion dollars seemed to be getting farther and farther away with every minute.

The phone rang.

Electro rushed across the room. Maybe it was Davis, telling him the charges were finally in place. Maybe it was the mayor, willing to resume negotiating in secret.

He picked up the phone. It was Stewart.

"Electro," the other man said. "I thought I'd give you a final call."

"Final?" Electro asked. "What's going on out there? I can't get in touch with Davis—"

"Mr. Davis is no longer working for us," Stewart purred into the phone. "He had divided loyalties, you see. It was a shame he never had a chance to rig the explosives in the old tunnel. Now I guess your master plan won't work at all, will it?"

"Why are you doing this?" Electro demanded. "You were going to get a lot out of this, too!"

"Ah, but this way, I get so much more," Stewart replied. "And I don't have a partner who'll shock me to death the first time I'm not looking. You see, Electro, this way Timilty is the hero. He's the one who foiled your blackmail plans. This guarantees his election. And having Timilty in office gives me far more than a measly hundred million dollars. You were planning to give me my finder's fee, weren't you, Electro?"

Stewart sighed. "Now, there's no blackmail, so I'll wave the finder's fee. After all, Tyler Stewart is always fair. I know it must be frustrating. Feel free to trash the place. I'm sure, once Timilty is elected, that the city will be honored to award me the contract to rebuild the pumping station.

"It's certainly been a pleasure doing business with you, Electro. Especially now that the business is over."

Tyler Stewart hung up on him midlaugh.

Electro stared at the silent phone. Tyler Stewart had stopped Davis from completing his job, destroying any chance for Electro's success, and then had used Timilty to give the media the information about the old pumping station on a silver platter.

Electro screamed.

Tyler Stewart had only one thing right.

Electro wanted to smash everything in sight.

Spider-Man had found his way up through the drainage tunnels until he heard voices nearby—the voices of the all-news station blaring in the control room. He had followed the sound and found himself immediately below a drainage grate in the middle of the master control room.

Above him, a phone was ringing.

He listened as Electro grew more and more angry. The volume on the cell phone had apparently been turned up to maximum, because he could make out just about all of what Tyler Stewart was saying, too. So now he had the whole sad story. His only remaining job was to keep Electro from destroying a multimillion-dollar facility.

Spidey popped up the grate on top of him and jumped out onto the control-room floor.

"Spider-Man?" Electro called. "What are you doing here?"

Boy, he loved it when the bad guys fed him straight lines. "I could have sworn the map said turn left at Albuquerque!" He waved at Electro. "But as long as I'm here, why don't the both of us take a trip downtown?"

"I've had enough of your stupid jokes, wall-crawler!" Electro shouted. "I'm going to fry you where you stand!"

Spidey jumped out of the way of a lethal bolt of electricity.

"Everybody's a critic," he muttered as he shot a line of webbing around a girder overhead.

The gleaming panel behind where he had stood a moment before now had a gaping hole in it the size of a Toyota. He remembered Electro's increased strength from their last couple of encounters. Even with his recuperative powers, his ribs were still a little sore from his too-close encounter with a couple of brick walls.

"You can't get away from me, Spider-Man!" Electro called. "I've had a really bad day. But killing you would make me feel a whole lot better!"

A second bolt of power almost caught him midair. He jumped from his web-strand, ducking under the lethal line of blazing white. This dodging of Electro's bolts just wasn't going to work. Electro was far more powerful than Spider-Man, and sooner or later, one of those bolts was going to connect. He had to distract his opponent somehow, maybe outwit him into trapping himself. Spider-Man jumped from the floor to a wall.

"Got you!" he called, slapping a wad of webbing around Electro's ankles.

Electro swayed in surprise, almost falling. He glared up at Spider-Man.

"Is this the best you can do? A single jolt of my power will burn the webbing away."

The webbing dissolved under a single fine line of sparks from Electro's fingertips.

"Got you again!" Spider-Man said as he stuck another gooey gob on Electro's backside, attaching him to the control board behind him.

"What are you doing?" Electro shrieked. "Trying to make me madder?"

"If I was," Spider-Man answered, "apparently I'm succeeding."

"Even behind me, this is nothing more than an inconvenience." Electro frowned in concentration. "I just have to direct a quick surge of power down around my—"

Spider-Man launched himself from the wall, somersaulting in midair. Electro looked up when he was only three feet away.

"Wha—"

Spider-Man's boot connected solidly with Electro's jaw. Then he rolled on the floor, bouncing up and onto the far wall.

Electro was on his back. Maybe he'd actually knocked the bad guy out.

Electro groaned.

Oh, well, Spidey thought. *No such luck.* Maybe he could swoop in again and finish him off.

But Electro was already back on his feet. "Is that the best you can do, Spider-Man? No one can compete with my power!" he shrieked, unleashing a huge bolt of energy with both hands.

Spider-Man got out of the way. The wall was not so lucky. A twenty-foot square of concrete and steel evaporated.

A wall of water came cascading into the room. Electro must have destroyed one of the walls that led directly to the tunnels that fed the pumps.

Ten feet of water filled the room in ten seconds. Spider-Man was able to cling to the ceiling, still well above the raging waters.

Electro was not so lucky. His electrical might was no match for ten thousand gallons of water. The water served to, in essence, short-circuit him and render him insensate. Then the vast weight of the water overwhelmed him.

"This is a WNN bulletin!"

Betty Brant and Ben Urich both looked up at the monitor. Ben had gotten back to the *Bugle* only a few moments before. His other leads hadn't panned out. He was glad Peter had made it back in one piece; you couldn't be a photographer for the *Bugle* and not know how to take care of yourself. Betty was about to tell Ben what she and Mary Jane—well, Mary Jane mostly—had found, but the bulletin interrupted her. Something was happening down at the power station.

"This is Steve Roman, on the scene in Yonkers. The electrical force field that has prevented any entry into the

Yonkers pumping plant has suddenly vanished, and New York City's elite Code Blue unit is about to try entering the facility and confront Electro."

The picture bobbed up and down wildly as the reporter spun around. "Wait a minute. Something's happening down the hill, toward the river. It's Spider-Man!"

The picture cut to a different camera, this one zooming into a close-up of Spider-Man carrying someone through the woods.

"Wait a second!" the reporter cried. "Spidey's carrying—yes, he's carrying Electro! I have word that the Code Blue forces are leaving the fence behind me and coming down to confront Spider-Man now."

The camera watched as Spider-Man walked up to the edge of the crowd and very gently lowered the unconscious Electro, wrapped in a web cocoon, to the ground.

"Here's your blackmailer," Spider-Man said. "I think someone should call the Vault and tell them they've got a new guest."

Three cops, their guns drawn, walked in from the right-hand side of the screen.

"Spider-Man!" one of them called. "Stop right there!"

Spider-Man didn't make a move.

"We don't want to shoot you, Spider-Man," the cop in the middle said. "But you're wanted in connection with the murder of Michael Luce. We need you to surrender and come with us."

"I had nothing to do with Luce's murder," Spider-Man said.

"That very well may be," the cop replied, "but you're still wanted for questioning."

"Sorry," Spidey replied. "I can't. Not until I clear my name."

"Then we're going to have to bring you down," the cop replied. He looked to the two other officers. "Get out of the way. Code Blue will take it from here!"

But Spider-Man was already gone.

"Wow," Ben whistled. "Just a little tension." He looked over at Betty. "This can't last. Spider-Man's either going to have to go into hiding, or turn himself in. Otherwise, the guys in Code Blue are going to kill him."

"I think we may have another solution," Betty replied with a smile.

"We do?" Ben asked.

"Come with me," Betty replied. "I want you to meet Fast Anthony Davis."

Eighteen

M ary Jane hoped this was the answer.

She had brought Anthony Davis out of the alley and met up again with Betty. Together, the three of them had gone to the locker at the Mailboxes Etc. where Davis had stashed the disposable camera that he had used as insurance on the night Michael Luce was murdered. Then they returned to the *Bugle,* Davis in tow.

Ben and Robbie had joined them as the lab technician quickly developed the roll and produced a contact sheet.

Robbie held up the black sheet with the small, film-size images of every shot on the roll. He nodded. "This stuff looks like dynamite." He turned to the technician. "I need prints of three, seven, eleven, and twelve." He frowned back at the sheet. "Give me one and two, also."

The technician nodded and hustled back into the dark-room.

Several tense minutes later, they had the photos in their hands. The first photo showed Timilty, with Luce and the burly man that Davis identified as Andy, all standing in the warehouse. There were a couple of early shots of Spidey fighting the crooks in the rafters.

Mary Jane frowned. "These are a little blurry."

Davis shrugged. "Hey, sue me."

"You can still see what's happening," Ben said. "I think these will go a long ways toward clearing Spider-Man."

"Not to mention throwing a monkey wrench in Timilty's campaign," Betty agreed. "These photos show he's right in the middle of this. At the very least, he's a witness to Michael Luce's murder."

"Timilty's got a lot of explaining to do," Robbie agreed. "And the *Bugle*'s just the paper to make him do it."

There was more, including a shot of Andy sticking a knife in Luce's back, with a shocked Brian Timilty standing beside him.

"I think we just got the front-page photo for an extra edition," Robbie said.

This is great, MJ thought. *These photos will clear Peter for sure.* It felt good to save Spider-Man.

"So what do I get out of all of this?" Fast Anthony called from where he sat glowering in the corner.

"You've been very helpful," Betty said. "Whatever

happens, you'll have the backing of one of New York's major newspapers."

"We'll pay you for these, too," Robbie added. "We'll give you the *Bugle*'s top rate. That will pay your rent for a month or two."

"Well," Davis admitted, "this wasn't exactly what I had in mind. But if I don't do something to blow the whistle, I could wind up very dead." He pointed at the man with the knife in the photo. "I know Andy all too well. And, worse, Andy knows me."

"I'm going to put a call in to the DA," Betty said. "I'm pretty sure Tower can be talked into cutting you a deal—your story for a spot in the Witness Protection Program."

Davis thought about it for about two seconds. "Hey, it'll keep me alive. Right now, that sounds like the best deal of all."

"Sounds good," Robbie agreed. He waved the photos in his hand. "I'll clear these with Jonah."

"Is there going to be a problem?" Mary Jane asked. She knew J. Jonah Jameson didn't like being proven wrong, and these photos would show him that the man Jonah had practically canonized was directly involved in the murder of his own campaign manager.

"With Jonah?" Robbie grinned. "No. He'll fume, rant, and rave, try to blame Spider-Man for all of it, and generally carry on like trash for fifteen minutes, but once he gets that out of his system, he'll go for it. This is big news, after all."

* * *

The Rhino didn't know how long he could take this.

At least he'd seen a little action in the Diamond District. Not that it had turned out all that great. Code Blue had blasted him. Whatever they had used had knocked the wind out of him and thrown him back twenty feet.

The Rhino winced when he remembered how much it had stung the first day or so. Now, besides a little bruise on his chest, he would be fine. But when he'd been pushed off his feet by that blast, he'd lost all the diamonds. Every one of them had been recovered by the police.

Jobs sometimes went wrong. You had to expect it. But the crazy part was that Stewart's men hadn't even seemed upset.

"Hey," Devlin had said with a grin when the Rhino had climbed back in the van. "You tried. This was kind of a trial. Stewart will need you for something else." The van, still covered with its police markings, had left the scene unchallenged, and they had come back to the motel room, and the watchful eyes of Spike and Jeremiah.

Then they just sat there some more. The Rhino's opinion that this was as bad as prison had changed; this was worse.

There had been no news of the something else that Devlin had mentioned—nothing, really, besides Spike and his endless gin rummy games. At least Spike liked to talk. In the time that he'd been held in this motel room, the Rhino figured he now knew every aspect of Stewart's operation. Not that it would do him any good.

At least he didn't have to see that much of that giggling moron. Maybe someday, when he really needed exercise, he would break Andy's neck. The Rhino sighed. He guessed that proved he could still be passionate about something.

As for the rest of it—even the robbery in the Diamond District—his heart just wasn't in it anymore. Whatever he had to do, he just wanted to get the money from Stewart and get out of here.

The Rhino sighed again. He'd learned patience from all that time spent in the joint. He could wait a little longer.

The phone rang. Spike answered it and talked for a moment. He nodded to the Rhino as soon as he had hung up.

"That was Stewart. He wants you now."

As a rule, Tyler Stewart didn't like to gloat. But even he had to admit that he had played the members of this little drama brilliantly. Michael Luce, the man who knew the most about his checkered past, was dead. Brian Timilty, a man who was so scared he would do anything Stewart asked, was guaranteed to be the next mayor of New York City. Spider-Man, the super hero most likely to have given Stewart trouble, had a price on his head thanks to the *Daily Bugle,* and was such a wanted man that police had almost gunned him down. Electro had played his part brilliantly, falling right into Stewart's trap before he was sent back to prison. Sure, Davis knew the score, too, but Andy would make sure he never talked.

It was almost perfect. The one potential problem was that hothead Spider-Man. He had surprised Stewart by going after Electro even when the police had orders to bring him in at any cost. If Spider-Man and Electro had exchanged any words during their battle, it was very likely that Spidey would have discovered who was behind it all.

And that meant he would be coming for Stewart next.

Now it was time for Stewart to bring in his extra protection. He made the call, and had his men bring the Rhino in from the motel. Should Spider-Man be foolish enough to show up here, the Rhino and Stewart's gunmen would keep him busy—at least until Stewart did his civic duty and called the police in to capture him. Or perhaps the Rhino could see his way to ridding the world of that costumed menace called Spider-Man once and for all. After all that Spider-Man had done, it would clearly be self-defense. The Rhino and Tyler Stewart could end up as heroes.

You didn't need super powers to succeed in New York. You just needed a super brain.

The phone rang. It was Devlin, telling him he and Andy had the Rhino downstairs.

"Well, bring him on up. And get his costume, too."

He wanted the Rhino ready for the big battle.

A moment later, the big man stood before Stewart in his office. And big he was, dwarfing both Devlin and Andy, who stood to either side.

"I've been quite pleased with the small jobs you've

done for me so far," Stewart said, "but now I need you for the most important job of all."

The Rhino barely nodded at Stewart's greeting. He stood there, unmoving, regarding Stewart from the other side of the desk. Stewart felt like someone had moved a mountain into the middle of his office.

"You know what's going on with Spider-Man," Stewart began.

The Rhino shook his head.

"What?" Stewart asked. "You haven't been watching the news?"

"Hey, you know, boss," Devlin said with a smirk. "Jeremiah and his movies?"

"All the time?" Stewart asked.

"All the time," the Rhino rumbled.

Andy giggled as he played with his knife. The Rhino turned his glare in Andy's direction for an instant before he turned back to Stewart.

Stewart decided he'd better finish his explanation. "Well, if you had, you would know that Spider-Man's wanted by the police. What you wouldn't know is that Spider-Man and I have, well, shall I say, little differences? And these differences might make him come after me.

"So here's where you come in. If Spider-Man does show up here, and I think he will, you are to use any force necessary to subdue him so that we can deliver him to the cops, either dead or alive."

"You want me to fight Spider-Man?" the Rhino rumbled.

"If he attacks here, yes." Stewart waved to Devlin. "Tom, why don't you go get his costume?"

Devlin nodded and left the room.

"I don't know about Spider-Man," the Rhino continued. "I've been in this business too long. I'm tired of getting my butt kicked by every super hero in town. Getting beat up by Spider-Man over and over—it gets embarrassing. If it's all the same to you, I'll sit this one out."

Stewart couldn't believe this. "What? What do you think I hired you to do, sit in a motel room? I know you want money to get away from here. I have that money, and I will pay you well. But you must protect me from Spider-Man long enough for me to call in the cops. So you may get your butt kicked. So you may even have to go to jail. I've got good lawyers. They'll get you out in no time. And once you're back out, I'll make sure you get enough money so that you never have to work again."

Tom Devlin stepped back into the room, accompanied by two other men whom Stewart had summoned by pressing a hidden buzzer.

"Besides," Stewart continued, "until you get your costume on, you're not in much of a position to argue."

The Rhino turned to see Andy, Devlin, and the two newcomers all pointing guns his way.

"All right," the Rhino rumbled. "I'll do it." He grabbed the suit from Devlin's outstretched arm.

"Tom?" Stewart offered with a smile. He knew he could get even a depressed super-villain to see the light of day. Tyler Stewart had enough guns and money to have anybody see the light. "Why don't you take the Rhino into the next room so he can—"

He was interrupted by the sound of breaking glass.

Stewart whirled around.

Spider-Man had come in through the window.

Nineteen

The Rhino decided this was totally screwed up.

First, Stewart had broken him out of jail, without even asking if he had wanted to be freed. Then Stewart had stuck him in a hotel room for days, with only a couple of senseless jobs to break the monotony. And now this?

Stewart's goons opened fire.

"No!" Stewart cried. "Not here! Not in my office!"

That only seemed to make the goons shoot even more. Not that any of their bullets were getting anywhere near Spider-Man. Devlin went down first, felled by a blow to the stomach by the wall-crawler. Spidey turned his attention to the two newer gunmen as two more rushed in through the doorway.

The Rhino heard Andy giggling softly behind him. He

looked around and saw Stewart's assassin aiming his Magnum right at the middle of Spider-Man's back.

The Rhino had been wanting to do this for a long time. He charged straight at the startled Andy, smashing him hard against a cherry-paneled wall. Andy moaned once, then collapsed like a rag doll.

He turned to look at Spider-Man, who had knocked down and trussed up the remaining gunmen in the time the Rhino's back was turned. The Rhino held up his hands.

"I'm not looking for a fight with you, wall-crawler. I didn't want any part of this to begin with." He nodded down at the crumpled Andy. "That was personal."

"Oh," Spider-Man said after a moment. "Thanks."

Wow, Rhino thought. *No clever quip? I actually shut Spider-Man up for once?*

The Rhino smiled.

No, Stewart thought, *this can't be happening.* He had planned too long and hard.

Spider-Man walked toward him.

"It's over, Stewart."

"What's over?" Stewart demanded. "I was only trying to protect myself from a known fugitive. What have you got on me?"

"I know you're responsible for the murder of Michael Luce."

"How could you know that?" Stewart laughed derisively. "How could you prove something like that? It's your word against mine, Spider-Man, and, as far as this city is concerned, *you're* the killer on the loose."

Spider-Man stopped and stared at Stewart. Faintly, through the broken window, Stewart could hear police sirens approaching.

Yes, Tyler Stewart thought. *I still have the upper hand.*

"What are you going to do to me, Spider-Man?" he taunted. "Hit me? As much as you'd probably like to, even you realize this is one problem that can't be solved with your fists."

The sirens stopped just below the window. Stewart could hear half a dozen car doors slam as the police rushed into the building from the street below.

Spider-Man took a step away, as if he would jump through the window.

"I'm Mr. Money, Spider-Man," Stewart jeered. "A cornerstone of the community. What are they going to do to me? You'd better run. You're a wanted man, a murderer. Run for the rest of your life."

The Rhino placed a huge hand on Stewart's shoulder.

"I'm not running any more," the large man said. "I want to have a life."

Spider-Man regarded the large man for a minute. "For once, Rhino, I agree with you. I've got a life, too. I'm innocent. I'm going to wait for the police and take my chances."

No, Stewart thought, *this wasn't how it was supposed to work.* It would be so much easier to twist the story his way if Spider-Man was running.

But wait—why panic? Even with Spider-Man here, Stewart was still the respected citizen, while this costumed clown was wanted for murder. The police were sure to see it his way.

The phone rang. Stewart's man downstairs told him the police were here. Stewart told them to send them on up.

To Stewart's surprise, District Attorney Tower was in the lead. He was followed by two men in rumpled suits whom the DA introduced as Detectives Briscoe and Logan. They were followed by six uniformed police who were not introduced.

"I surrender," the Rhino announced as soon as the introductions were over. "I never wanted to be here in the first place."

"Okay," Tower said. He nodded to a couple of the uniforms. "Why don't we take him downstairs?" He looked at Stewart's men, unconscious or trussed up with webbing on the floor. "Why don't we get these folks out of here, too? I'm sure they have some interesting stories to tell."

"You got here just in time," Stewart said. "Spider-Man was going to kill me!"

Tower glanced over at Spider-Man. "That reminds me. Spider-Man, we will have to talk. But I don't believe we'll be filing any charges. We've gotten some very interesting information, thanks to Betty Brant down at the *Bugle.*"

"What?" Stewart was almost screaming. "What are you doing? What's the meaning of this! Spider-Man's a murderer! He was going to kill me!"

Tower glanced at the detectives behind him. "Detective Briscoe? Why don't you do the honors?"

The other detective stepped forward with a pair of handcuffs.

"Tyler Stewart," Briscoe began. "You are under arrest for conspiracy to commit murder. You have the right to remain silent . . ."

Epilogue

What a difference a week made!

Spider-Man sailed across midtown Manhattan, swinging from one building to the next. The day was clear and warm. He felt as free as the birds that flew in his path.

After Briscoe had arrested Stewart, the evidence had come pouring in. Fast Anthony Davis had talked first about the photographs. Then the Rhino had testified about what had really happened between Spider-Man and Tyler Stewart. Even Electro, from his special cell in the Vault, had implicated Stewart in every stage of his pumping-station blackmail plan. Just yesterday, a grand jury had indicted Stewart, not just for Luce's murder, but for his part in Electro's blackmail scheme. It looked like most of Stewart's mob was going to go away for a long time, too, especially the man shown knifing Luce in Davis's photos. Fast Anthony Davis had been whisked into the Witness Protection Program. And the Rhino was sharing his knowledge of the Stewart organization, in return for a commuted sentence.

District Attorney Tower was holding a press conference at City Hall this very minute. Spidey had meant to get there on time, but it just felt so good to be able to swing through the city without someone trying to shoot him down that he was in danger of missing it. Still, he thought he would pop in for a minute through the window. Everybody thought he was a hero again. He could stand a little boost to his spirits.

He swung onto the windowsill.

"Ladies and gentlemen of the press," Tower was saying from the front of the room. "This whole case would not have been solved without the superb investigative reporting of the staff of the *Daily Bugle*. Two of the reporters primarily responsible for cracking this case, Betty Brant and Ben Urich, are on this podium with me today."

J. Jonah Jameson, who sat next to Betty and Ben on the podium, stood at that. "I can't tell you how proud we at the *Bugle* are of our fine staff. And do not forget that I, the *Bugle*'s crusading publisher, have always encouraged my staff to root out corruption and falsehood, whether they find it on the street or in the boardroom."

"I don't think anybody's going to forget about you, Jonah," Tower remarked. All the reporters laughed. "But I see that Spider-Man has finally joined us. Why don't you come to the front of the room, Spider-Man, while I finish my remarks?"

All heads turned as Spidey bounded to the front of the room. Jonah looked like someone had punched him in the gut, but the publisher, for once, said nothing.

"Parts of our investigation are still ongoing, including Brian Timilty's alleged association with organized crime, and the extent of his participation in the murder of his campaign chief, Michael Luce. As most of you already know, earlier today Brian Timilty withdrew from the mayoral race, claiming that he would devote his time to clearing his name. He will have plenty of opportunity to do so. He has already been subpoenaed by the grand jury, and I understand that federal investigators wish to talk to him as well."

Tower smiled at Spider-Man as he took his place on the stage, right next to J. Jonah Jameson. "My staff has given me further good news. The man wounded in the bank plaza incident, Mr. John Garcia, is now out of his coma and is expected to make a full recovery. Which brings me to the reason I asked Spider-Man to join us."

Garcia's out of the coma? That was another great relief. No matter how it had happened, Spider-Man couldn't help but blame himself for the man's injury.

He turned to Jameson. "Hey, Jonah," he whispered. "You and me, on the same stage together, being honored side by side. I could get used to this."

Jonah glared at him.

"As you know," Tower continued, "a cornerstone of

Timilty's campaign was to spread fear and distrust of super heroes. As we can see, through Spider-Man's selfless actions, in apprehending Electro and assisting with the capture of Tyler Stewart, nothing could be further from the truth. Spider-Man is one hero this city can trust. He's proven it over and over throughout the years, and I and the city of New York would like to thank him for it."

The whole room broke out in applause.

"Wow," Spider-Man whispered to Jonah. "We should do this again sometime. Maybe you and I can start seeing each other socially."

Spidey waved to the crowd as Jameson turned beet red.

He looked down and saw Mary Jane sitting in the first row. Betty stepped off the podium and went over to talk to her as Tower asked if there were any questions.

"You deserve to be up there, too," Betty said. "And where's Peter? He deserves these accolades as much as anybody."

"Peter's a little shy," MJ said.

Betty nodded and laughed. "That's kind of refreshing, considering all the egos already in this room."

"Spider-Man can get all the glory," MJ agreed. "Peter just needs to get that paycheck."

Well, Spider-Man had had enough glory for one day. He waved a final time to the reporters as he jumped to the window and swung out into the glorious, sun-filled New York afternoon.

CHRONOLOGY TO THE MARVEL NOVELS AND ANTHOLOGIES

What follows is a guide to the order in which the Marvel novels and short stories published by Byron Preiss Multimedia Company and Boulevard Books take place in relation to each other. Please note that this is not a hard-and-fast chronology, but a guideline that is subject to change at authorial or editorial whim. This list covers all the novels and anthologies published from October 1994 to December 1998.

The short stories are each given an abbreviation to indicate which anthology the story appeared in. USM = *The Ultimate Spider-Man,* USS = *The Ultimate Silver Surfer,* USV = *The Ultimate Super-Villains,* UXM = *The Ultimate X-Men,* and UTS = *Untold Tales of Spider-Man.*

If you have any questions or comments regarding this chronology, please write us. Snail mail: Keith R.A. De-Candido, Marvel Novels Editor, Byron Preiss Multimedia Company, Inc., 24 West 25th Street, New York, New York, 10010-2710. E-mail: KRAD@IX.NETCOM.COM.

—Keith R.A. DeCandido, Editor

"The Silver Surfer" **[flashback]** by Tom DeFalco and Stan Lee [USS]
The Silver Surfer's origin. The early parts of this flash-

back start several decades, possibly several centuries, ago, and continue to a point just prior to "To See Heaven in a Wild Flower."

"Spider-Man" by Stan Lee and Peter David [USM]
   A retelling of Spider-Man's origin.

"Side by Side with the Astonishing Ant-Man!" by Will Murray [UTS]
"Suits" by Tom De Haven and Dean Wesley Smith [USM]
"After the First Death . . ." by Tom DeFalco [UTS]
"Celebrity" by Christopher Golden and José R. Nieto [UTS]
"Better Looting Through Modern Chemistry" by John Garcia and Pierce Askegren [UTS]
   These stories take place very early in Spider-Man's career.

"To the Victor" by Richard Lee Byers [USV]
   Most of this story takes place in an alternate timeline, but the jumping-off point is here.

"To See Heaven in a Wild Flower" by Ann Tonsor Zeddies [USS]
"Point of View" by Len Wein [USS]
   These stories take place shortly after the end of the flashback portion of "The Silver Surfer."

"**Identity Crisis**" by Michael Jan Friedman [UTS]

"**The Liar**" by Ann Nocenti [UTS]

"**The Doctor's Dilemma**" by Danny Fingeroth [UTS]

"**Moving Day**" by John S. Drew [UTS]

"**Deadly Force**" by Richard Lee Byers [UTS]

"**Improper Procedure**" by Keith R.A. DeCandido [USS]

"**Poison in the Soul**" by Glenn Greenberg [UTS]

"**The Ballad of Fancy Dan**" by Ken Grobe and Steven A. Roman [UTS]

"**Do You Dream in Silver?**" by James Dawson [USS]

"**Livewires**" by Steve Lyons [UTS]

"**Arms and the Man**" by Keith R.A. DeCandido [UTS]

"**Incident on a Skyscraper**" by Dave Smeds [USS]

These all take place at various and sundry points in the careers of Spider-Man and the Silver Surfer, after their origins, but before Spider-Man married and the Silver Surfer ended his exile on Earth.

"**Cool**" by Lawrence Watt-Evans [USM]

"**Blindspot**" by Ann Nocenti [USM]

"**Tinker, Tailor, Soldier, Courier**" by Robert L. Washington III [USM]

"**Thunder on the Mountain**" by Richard Lee Byers [USM]

"**The Stalking of John Doe**" by Adam-Troy Castro [UTS]

These all take place just prior to Peter Parker's marriage to Mary Jane Watson.

"On the Beach" by John J. Ordover [USS]

  This story takes place just prior to the Silver Surfer's release from imprisonment on Earth.

Daredevil: Predator's Smile by Christopher Golden

"Disturb Not Her Dream" by Steve Rasnic Tem [USS]

"My Enemy, My Savior" by Eric Fein [UTS]

"Kraven the Hunter is Dead, Alas" by Craig Shaw Gardner [USM]

"The Broken Land" by Pierce Askegren [USS]

"Radically Both" by Christopher Golden [USM]

"Godhood's End" by Sharman DiVono [USS]

"Scoop!" by David Michelinie [USM]

"Sambatyon" by David M. Honigsberg [USS]

"Cold Blood" by Greg Cox [USM]

"The Tarnished Soul" by Katherine Lawrence [USS]

"The Silver Surfer" [framing sequence] by Tom DeFalco and Stan Lee [USS]

  These all take place shortly after Peter Parker's marriage to Mary Jane Watson and shortly after the Silver Surfer attained his freedom from imprisonment on Earth.

Fantastic Four: To Free Atlantis by Nancy A. Collins

"If Wishes Were Horses" by Tony Isabella and Bob Ingersoll [USV]

CHRONOLOGY

"The Deviant Ones" by Glenn Greenberg [USV]
"An Evening in the Bronx with Venom" by John Gregory Betancourt and Keith R.A. DeCandido [USM]
These two stories take place one after the other, and a few months prior to The Venom Factor.

The Incredible Hulk: What Savage Beast by Peter David
This novel takes place over a one-year period, starting here and ending just prior to Rampage.

"On the Air" by Glenn Hauman [UXM]
"Connect the Dots" by Adam-Troy Castro [USV]
"Summer Breeze" by Jenn Saint-John and Tammy Lynne Dunn [UXM]
"Out of Place" by Dave Smeds [UXM]
These stories all take place prior to the Mutant Empire *trilogy.*

X-Men: Mutant Empire Book 1: *Siege* by Christopher Golden
X-Men: Mutant Empire Book 2: *Sanctuary* by Christopher Golden
X-Men: Mutant Empire Book 3: *Salvation* by Christopher Golden
These three novels take place within a three-day period.

"The Love of Death or the Death of Love" by Craig Shaw Gardner [USS]

"Firetrap" by Michael Jan Friedman [USV]

"What's Yer Poison?" by Christopher Golden and José R. Nieto [USS]

"Sins of the Flesh" by Steve Lyons [USV]

"Doom²" by Joey Cavalieri [USV]

"Child's Play" by Robert L. Washington III [USV]

"A Game of the Apocalypse" by Dan Persons [USS]

"All Creatures Great and Skrull" by Greg Cox [USV]

"Ripples" by José R. Nieto [USV]

"Who Do You Want Me to Be?" by Ann Nocenti [USV]

"One for the Road" by James Dawson [USV]

These stories are more or less simultaneous, with "Child's Play" taking place shortly after "What's Yer Poison?" and "A Game of the Apocalypse" taking place shortly after "The Love of Death or the Death of Love."

"Five Minutes" by Peter David [USM]

This takes place on Peter Parker and Mary Jane Watson-Parker's first anniversary.

Spider-Man: The Venom Factor by Diane Duane

Spider-Man: The Lizard Sanction by Diane Duane

Spider-Man: The Octopus Agenda by Diane Duane

These three novels take place within a six-week period.

"The Night I Almost Saved Silver Sable" by Tom De-
Falco [USV]
"Traps" by Ken Grobe [USV]
These stories take place one right after the other.

Iron Man: The Armor Trap by Greg Cox
Iron Man: Operation A.I.M. by Greg Cox
"Private Exhibition" by Pierce Askegren [USV]
Fantastic Four: Redemption of the Silver Surfer by
Michael Jan Friedman
Spider-Man and The Incredible Hulk: Rampage (**Doom's
Day Book 1**) by Danny Fingeroth and Eric Fein
Spider-Man and Iron Man: Sabotage (**Doom's Day Book
2**) by Pierce Askegren and Danny Fingeroth
Spider-Man and Fantastic Four: Wreckage (**Doom's Day
Book 3**) by Eric Fein and Pierce Askegren
The Incredible Hulk: Abominations by Jason Henderson
Operation A.I.M. *takes place about two weeks after* The
Armor Trap. *The "Doom's Day" trilogy takes place within
a three-month period. The events of* Operation A.I.M.,
"Private Exhibition," Redemption of the Silver Surfer, *and*
Rampage *happen more or less simultaneously.* Wreckage *is
only a few months after* The Octopus Agenda. Abomina-
tions *takes place shortly after the end of* Wreckage.

"It's a Wonderful Life" by eluki bes shahar [UXM]
"Gift of the Silver Fox" by Ashley McConnell [UXM]
"Stillborn in the Mist" by Dean Wesley Smith [UXM]

"Order from Chaos" by Evan Skolnick [UXM]
These stories take place simultaneously.

"X-Presso" by Ken Grobe [UXM]
"Life Is But a Dream" by Stan Timmons [UXM]
"Four Angry Mutants" by Andy Lane and Rebecca Levene [UXM]
"Hostages" by J. Steven York [UXM]
These stories take place one right after the other.

Spider-Man: Carnage in New York by David Michelinie and Dean Wesley Smith
Spider-Man: Goblin's Revenge by Dean Wesley Smith
These novels take place one right after the other.

X-Men: Smoke and Mirrors by eluki bes shahar
This novel takes place three and a half months after "It's a Wonderful Life."

Generation X by Scott Lobdell and Elliot S! Maggin
X-Men: The Jewels of Cyttorak by Dean Wesley Smith
X-Men: Empire's End by Diane Duane
X-Men: Law of the Jungle by Dave Smeds
X-Men: Prisoner X by Ann Nocenti
These novels take place one right after the other.

Fantastic Four: Countdown to Chaos by Pierce Askegren
Generation X: Crossroads by J. Steven York

Captain America: Liberty's Torch by Tony Isabella & Bob
    Ingersoll
*   These novels are more or less simultaneous.*

"Mayhem Party" by Robert Sheckley [USV]
*   This story takes place after* Goblin's Revenge.

X-Men and Spider-Man: Time's Arrow **Book 1:** *The Past*
    by Tom DeFalco and Jason Henderson
X-Men and Spider-Man: Time's Arrow **Book 2:** *The Present* by Tom DeFalco and Adam-Troy Castro
X-Men and Spider-Man: Time's Arrow **Book 3:** *The Future* by Tom DeFalco and eluki bes shahar
*   These novels take place within a twenty-four-hour period in the present, though it also involves traveling to various points in the past, to an alternate present, and to five
different alternate futures.*

Spider-Man: Valley of the Lizard by John Vornholt
Spider-Man: Venom's Wrath by Keith R.A. DeCandido
    and José R. Nieto
Spider-Man: Wanted Dead or Alive by Craig Shaw Gard-
ner
*   These novels take place one right after the other, with*
Venom's Wrath *a month after* Valley of the Lizard, *and*
Wanted Dead or Alive *several months after* Venom's Wrath.

X-Men: Codename Wolverine by Christopher Golden